Thank You

Thank You

Heartwarming stories
from BBC Radio 4's *Saturday Live*

FOREWORD BY REV. RICHARD COLES

PORTICO

First published in the United Kingdom in 2014 by
Portico
1 Gower Street
London
WC1E 6HD

An imprint of Pavilion Books Company Ltd

ISBN 978-1-90939-674-6

A CIP catalogue record for this book is available from
the British Library.

10 9 8 7 6 5 4 3 2 1

Reproduction by Mission Productions Ltd, Hong Kong
Printed and bound by Bookwell Ltd, Finland

This book can be ordered direct from the publisher
at www.pavilionbooks.com

CONTENTS

FOREWORD

Every once in a while in the *Saturday Live* studios
a great shout of 'Eureka!' is heard. Usually this is
just J.P. Devlin discovering where he's left his wad
of chewing baccy, but occasionally it is because
someone hits on a winning formula. The invention
of 'Inheritance Tracks' was such a moment, and
whoever's idea it was to ask a well-known person
to pick a piece of music that was the soundtrack to
their growing up, and another they would wish to
be the soundtrack to someone else's, helped earn
us our Sony Award.

The invention of 'Thank Yous' was another. It all
began when J.P., as is his wont, asked for your
stories of thank yous owed but unmade. I'm sure
you have your own: occasions when a stranger
helped you out but you never had the chance to
thank them for their kindness. I know you do,
actually, because the response was extraordinary
– not just the stories themselves but how they
touched our listeners – so extraordinary that we
held some over for the following week, and the
following week; by the fourth week we realised we
had a regular feature.

Not all are dramatic, like the story of the man whose valiant attempt at CPR on a 48-year-old motorcyclist was not enough to save his life, but was enough to ensure a successful organ donation, which saved the lives of three other people. Some are a bit more oblique (like so much on *Saturday Live*). I loved David's thank you to nameless university accommodation officers whose allocation of rooms in Halls of Residence have 'shaped countless lives and friendships' including his and his wife's – they met this way at Warwick in 1979.

Why do they move people so much? I think partly because gratitude is so unexpected in what can be a surprisingly thankless world, but mostly because they speak so powerfully of gratitude, of kindness, of generosity, of selflessness, offered for no particular reason other than wishing to add to the sum of human goodness.

Rev. Richard Coles

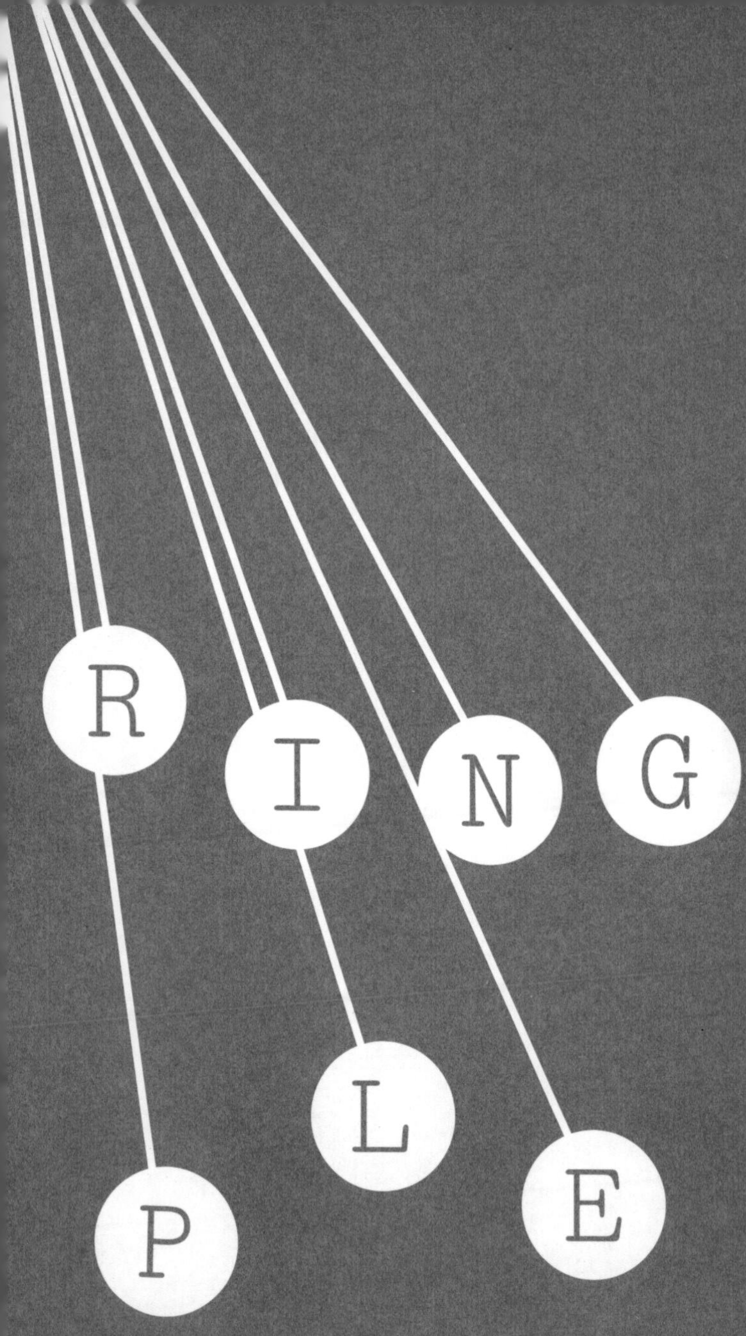
R I N G
L
E
P

'Thankfulness is
the beginning of
gratitude. Gratitude
is the completion
of thankfulness.
Thankfulness may consist
merely of words.
Gratitude is shown
in acts.'

HENRI FREDERIC AMIEL

The news is filled with stories
of people who have made life-
saving discoveries, overcome
incredible hardship, or
achieved amazing feats of
athleticism or endurance,
and they are certainly an
inspiration. But it is often
people we come into contact
with during the course of
our lives that have the
most profound effect on us:
from teachers who pass on
their passion for a subject,
neighbours who support us
through thick and thin,
medical staff who care for our
loved ones, or even strangers
who cheer us up when we are
miserable. In this collection
people say thank you to those
who have made a real difference
to them.

I left school with no O-levels but in 1985, while working for a holiday camp in Prestatyn in Wales, I met a man called Don who had recently been made redundant and he suggested that I go to college to get some qualifications. I took his advice and I started at college in September of that year and then completed a degree. I now have a good job in IT. I had very little back then and I'd like to shake his hand and tell him that I took his advice and made something of my life. You need a kick in the backside sometimes to move yourself up.

Huw, Conwy

In 1979 I married and went to live in Jamaica. Two years later my life seemed to be in tatters and I returned home. On the flight between Miami and Heathrow I sat next to a very funny Londoner. He took one look at me, with my face swollen from crying and eyes like slits, and instead of being put off he made some flippant remark like, 'Your holiday can't have been that bad!' which immediately made me laugh, and from then on he amused me. I'd like to thank him for that. He probably didn't know what he was doing at the time, he was probably doing it more to amuse himself than to cheer me up – but it was great fun.

Maria, Cornwall

I would like to thank Mr Makins who taught me English at the Municipal Grammar School in Wolverhampton in 1970. I can see now that he was quite a nervous young teacher, but I thought he had some really good ideas and it was in his class that I felt I was really good at something. He left the school after a couple of years and I'd like to say thank you. I'd like him to know that as a young adult I wrote several plays and a libretto; I later became an English teacher and now I'm a children's librarian. I'm sure I wouldn't have felt I was good enough to be an English teacher or to write a play if it hadn't been for his words.

Alison, West Midlands

I would like to thank Enid Castle, the headmistress at my secondary school. I had a difficult time at home and planned to leave as soon as I turned 16, but life became almost unbearable, and I didn't know how I would get through the Easter holidays. The Headmistress called me to her office and she said, 'I think the school should pay for you to go to Bordeaux for the Easter holidays', and she sent me on a school exchange so I didn't have to be at home. I made it through to my sixteenth birthday and then left home. What Enid Castle did that day was so simple and so desperately needed; she made all the difference at a crucial time.

Lydia, North Yorkshire

During my late 20s I was a patient at the Cassel Hospital in Surrey, where the staff and patients helped turn my life around. It was there that I met lecturer and art historian Laurence Bradbury. He came to the hospital to discuss art and gave us the confidence to voice our opinions. His influence has stayed with me ever since, and I'm quite comfortable now with visiting an art gallery and looking at the work on display, and then stepping back into my everyday life. Depression doesn't ever leave you completely but I'm much better able to handle it now.

Sally, Cambridgeshire

On 26 September 2013 my brother, Steve Gregory, was riding his motorbike on the A43 near Towcester, Northamptonshire, when witnesses saw him wobble slightly, pull over to the side of the road, drop his bike and then collapse. Several vehicles pulled over and people started to help him. He had no pulse, and a man called Jeremy began to perform CPR. Finally an air ambulance arrived and took Steve to hospital. With the help of the police I have been able to speak to and thank several of the people who were kind enough to help Steve, and all of them mentioned this man Jeremy who did the really effective CPR, which I understand was so effective that the emergency services found him to have regained a pulse. Sadly Steve had suffered a catastrophic brain haemorrhage and it was not possible to save his life, but because of the actions of all those present that morning, it meant that Steve, who was on the organ donor register, was a suitable donor. All I knew about this man Jeremy was that he was travelling to Sheffield to take his daughter to university. I have since had the pleasure of meeting Jeremy after managing to make contact with him, and I was able to thank him personally for acting so bravely and confidently. Although he wasn't able to save Steve's life, he did make a difference in that Steve was able to carry out his last gift of organ donation, and indirectly saved the lives of three other men through the donation of his two kidneys and his liver. Our family are so grateful to Jeremy, and it made losing Steve at only 48 so much more bearable.

Tina, Northamptonshire

I would like to say a huge, great big thank you to Jacquie Dinsdale. My long-term partner of 20-odd years was being treated for advanced prostate cancer and just before Christmas 2013, he said, 'I think we need to get married.' We arranged the wedding rather quickly and we hadn't saved for it, and Jacquie phoned me one morning and said, 'We're going to have the wedding reception in the village hall, and anybody that wants to come in the village can come along and pay £10 each, bring their own drinks and I'll cook the dinner.' She ended up cooking a three-course meal for 96 people. She arranged for the children in the village to wait at tables and help clear up and she really helped make our wedding a fantastic day.

Louise, North Yorkshire

I had a wonderful physics teacher. His name was Mr Frost and he taught at Longslade Upper School, Birstall, in Leicestershire. Not only did he teach me physics, but also spent many hours trying to convince me that physics was my subject. I didn't study it at the time but came back to it later through an Open University degree, and later still through a PhD. I'd love to be able to tell him that I did appreciate it even though I was a stupid teenager at the time.

Susan, Norfolk

I would like to thank my A-level English teacher. At the time he taught me I was awkward and uncooperative. It is only now, more than 20 years later, that I look back and I think that the things he taught me are still of value to me now. He will have known that I was quite a gifted student and I think he would have found it frustrating: he wrote in a school report just before my A-level, 'I only hope the A-level examiners will be more readily convinced of Giles' talent than I am.' When I got an A at A-level and distinction at scholarship level and I got a place at Oxford, he just said, 'I always knew you could.' I would like to thank him for looking past all that adolescent nonsense to teach so thankless a student as myself.

Giles, London

In about 1979 in Leyton, East London, I was recently divorced with two very young boys. Daphne Simkins lived below me in a two-up, two-down house. Times were very hard and Daphne would help me and understood exactly the predicament I was in. She was like another mum to me. I could tell her anything: I could open up to Daphne and she would listen. I still speak to her at least once a week and I treasure every contact with her. I can never thank her enough for that help she gave me in those early days. She will always mean the world to me.

Pauline, Hertfordshire

During my 30s I suffered quite a traumatic miscarriage. On this particular day I had been for a routine visit to the doctor but it had triggered memories of that terrible time and I was really upset. I was sitting in my car and had burst into tears when a woman walked by, knocked on the window, looked me right in the eyes and put her hand on my shoulder and said, 'I don't know what news you've received but no matter what it is I know you are going to be okay.' I have no idea who she was, and I thought it was so incredibly brave of her to do that, and it was what I needed to hear. I think of her every time I go to the doctor because I want to feel that shield of love and compassion around me.

Melanie, Essex

In 1968 a music teacher at my secondary school in Manchester played us *Vltava* by Smetana. I fell in love with it and my mum bought me the record. Thirty years later I had the privilege of sitting in Smetana Hall in Prague, at the opening night of the Spring Festival, listening to *Vltava* being played by the Czech Philharmonic Orchestra. I had a fantasy at the time of meeting this teacher and being able to say to her, 'I am here because of you.' Her name was Lesley Sinclair.

Sue, West Midlands

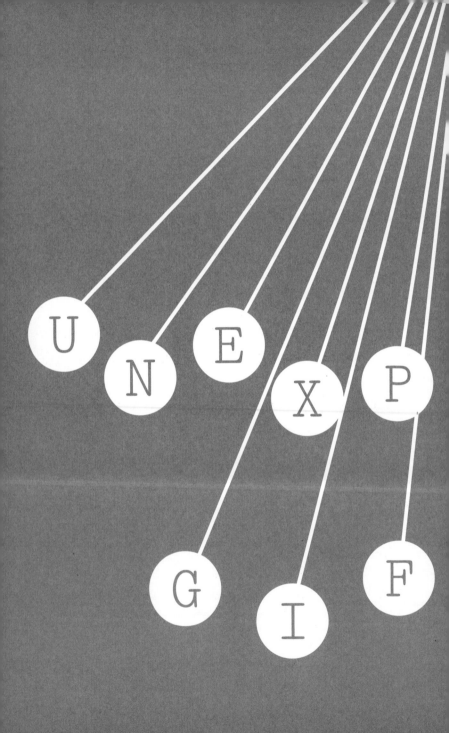

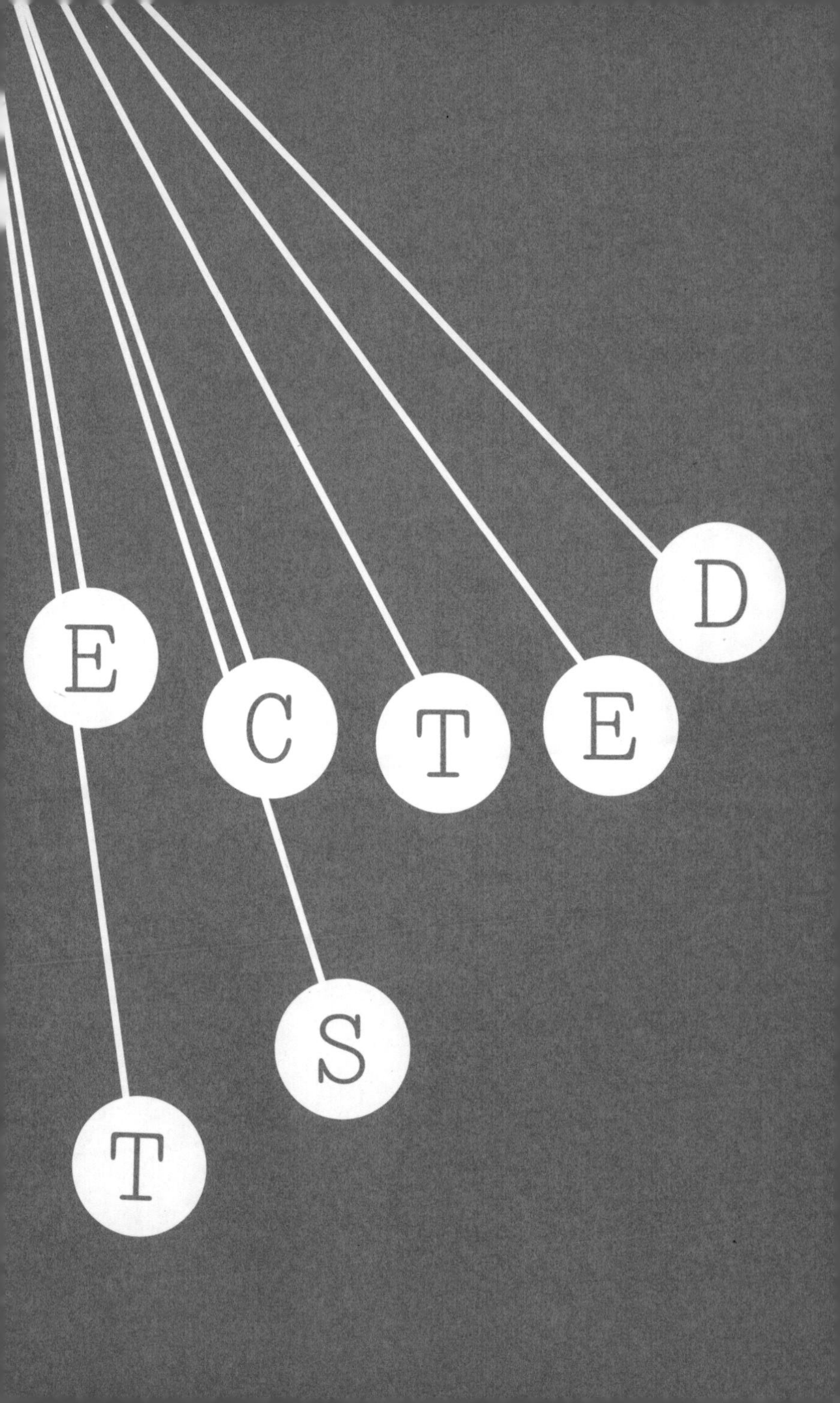
E
C
T
E
D
S
T

'I would maintain
that thanks are
the highest form
of thought, and
that gratitude is
happiness doubled
by wonder.'

G. K. CHESTERTON

Surprise presents from family or loved ones are always a treat, but what about gifts that come out of the blue from people we hardly know? Here is a compilation of stories about amazing acts of kindness, in many forms and both big and small: from free taxi rides and free lunches to accommodation and cinema tickets, and even a haggis. The generosity of strangers can be astonishing, with relatively large sums of money offered to those in need with no guarantee it will ever be paid back. It is no wonder that this collection of people wanted to say thank you.

My parents got married on 21 April 1940, at the West London Synagogue. On every anniversary of their wedding my mother used to tell me that, prior to theirs, there had been a society wedding. Being penniless refugees my parents' affair was to be very modest. Upon entering the synagogue for their own wedding, my parents found that the previous bride had left the floral decorations for them. Every wedding anniversary was special because my mother remembered the bride who had left the flowers for her. It was a wonderful gesture of loving kindness for all to take an example from.

Dani, London

In 1989 I had just moved to the outskirts of London. I hadn't made a social circle at the time, but I read an advert asking people to volunteer and stand and sell Marie Curie daffodils. I went into London, and I was given my tray and my tin, and was allocated Tottenham Court Road. On my way there, I was called across the road by a homeless man who was holding onto his pitch, and he tipped all the coins from his hat into his hand and insisted on being the first person to put money into my tin. It was such a contrast to all the busy shoppers who just walked past. On my way back I wanted to go and say thank you but he had moved on. After 20 years it still touches my heart that he did that.

Dee, Montgomeryshire

I received a call from a good friend of my late brother in February 2008. He said, 'Your brother is in hospital in the Intensive Care Unit; time is running out.' At the time I was estranged from my brother but I decided to get in the car and go. So, without planning and with no satnav, I went off to Wigan. Once I came off the motorway, I seemed to be driving for a very long time, and I couldn't see any relevant road signs. I saw a taxi company and went into the office and asked if I could hire a taxi so that I could follow it to the hospital. We arrived at the hospital, I got out to pay, and the driver would not take the money. She said 'I won't take it, I'm just pleased to help you out.' I managed to see my brother twice that week before he passed away. I would really like to thank those people who were so kind and helped me.

Wendy, Oxfordshire

* * * * * * * * * * * * * * * * * * *

In 1966 I was an engineering student in London. Someone I knew said he'd pay me to help him change the clutch on his car. I wore my oldest clothes and worked all day. By the time we finished I was filthy and freezing from lying on the ground. I didn't get paid that night and the only money I had was 3d [three old pence]. I went into a fish and chip shop on North End Road in West Kensington, London, and asked for 3d's worth of chips, and I thought the lady who was serving was going to say no, but instead she gave me the most enormous bag of chips I've ever seen. It had a really profound effect on me because it was a real show of compassion. Thank you very much.

Phil, Buckinghamshire

We'd like to thank the anonymous benefactor who left a copy of Rupert Brooke's 1914 poems and a copy of the latest Rupert Brooke biography in the Brooke Bar of The Pink and Lily at Lacey Green in the Chilterns. Rupert Brooke was such a regular customer that he wrote a poem called 'The Pink and Lily'. The staff have no idea who left the books and we'd like to say thank you.

Lara, Buckinghamshire

We were a group of National Servicemen in the RAF and were all demobbed at around the same time. My former billet mate, Tony Gallo, came from Edinburgh, and sent me a haggis as a sort of jokey house-warming present. My wife and I were young and had never seen a haggis before in our lives. We knew that there were some Scottish people living across the road, and so we went over and said, 'What do we have to do with this?' They told us how to cook it so we asked them to come and share it with us. The year after we had our first haggis party, they invited us over to their house for a repeat, and that was the start of a long tradition – in 2013 we celebrated our 50th anniversary party. Every year I think of Tony not realising he had started a lovely friendship. Thank you for the haggis Tony!

Brian, Warwickshire

We often think back nostalgically to August 1979 when, as impoverished students, we took our first holiday together as a couple. This was, of course, long before the days of the Internet so our forward planning consisted of nothing more than arming ourselves with a couple of bus tickets and a map. We headed from Newcastle upon Tyne to Victoria Coach Station in London and boarded a bus to Spain. After several days' travel we arrived in a town called Cartagena on a hot Monday afternoon. We were down to our last 100 pesetas (about £1) and set off to find a bank to cash a traveller's cheque. To our horror we discovered it was a bank holiday and were unable to access any cash. We spent the last of our money on a rather dry loaf of bread, and set off walking into the surrounding countryside, with no particular plan as to what we would do that night. We had walked for miles, and were becoming increasingly hungry, thirsty, tired and forlorn as night was falling. Then fate smiled upon us in the form of a peasant farmer who saw our plight, and invited us to his little cottage, which he shared with his wife and two small children. They obviously were quite poor but shared their evening meal with us and provided a bed for the night. They spoke no Spanish, only Catalan, which we did not understand, so communication was very difficult, and we were shy and unable to express our deep gratitude to them. So, after all these years, as a married couple with a little more cash than we had in 1979, we would like to at last say thank you for providing sanctuary all those years ago.

Brendan, County Wicklow, Ireland

In August 2008 my husband and I were on a
driving holiday in the Eifel region of Germany.
We were driving over the mountains and stopped
at a viewpoint, which was very beautiful, and met
another couple. We managed to strike up a bit of
a conversation, despite the fact that they couldn't
speak English, and we couldn't speak German. It
turned out they had a nephew who worked in Britain
quite close to where we lived. The gentleman
phoned his nephew, handed the phone to us, and
the nephew asked whether we would be interested
in going to see a local tourist site with them, which
we agreed to. We followed them in our car and
they took us to a beautiful monastery, where they
insisted on buying us lunch and a guide book, and
taking us around the monastery. We ended up
spending the whole afternoon with them. We have
since lost touch, but it was a wonderful afternoon
and a really lovely experience.

Jennie, Staffordshire

In 1961, I had just finished as an au pair in Finland, and the only method of getting home was to catch a ferry from Copenhagen to Leith. I had travelled on the overnight ferry to Stockholm and found myself sitting and waiting for the trans-European express in Stockholm station for 13 hours. I had no money and I couldn't go anywhere, and I was stupidly wearing high heels and carrying three suitcases. A tall (I seem to remember he was quite good looking!) Englishman sat next to me, the first British person I'd spoken to in three months. He took pity on me, and bought me a sandwich and a cup of tea, and that was the only thing I had to eat in 36 hours. So, to the tall, blond, blazer-wearing Englishman, thank you.

Rhona, Fife

I was nine months pregnant and I knew my second baby was imminent. I had a strong urge to go out and have a spot of fun before the birth, so I squeezed my bump behind the steering wheel of my car, and took myself off to the cinema. The ticket machine wouldn't dispense my ticket so I asked for some help. The manager, John, came to my aid and told me that I had come to the wrong cinema (there are three in my home town) and that this showing was full. I sat down rather dejectedly, knowing there was no way I could get across town to the other cinema with my enormous tummy. John asked me to wait a moment and when he returned he slipped a ticket into my hand. He told me that one or two seats were always kept free. 'Don't tell anyone,' he said, and disappeared before I could thank him properly. The film was *Sex and the City* – at the time all my trousers were elasticated and high heels were a thing of the past, so I was craving a spot of glamour and silliness. Three days later I gave birth to my second daughter. I'd like to thank John properly for his kindness.

Emma, Cambridgeshire

When I was 20 years old, I woke up one morning and found out that I had been paralysed from the waist down and was admitted to Walsgrave Hospital in Coventry. There was no explanation as to what had happened to me, so I was feeling a bit down; my hair looked awful and I felt awful. A doctor came in one day, he was a registrar, and he looked at me and said 'I know exactly what will help you', and walked off. I thought 'I wonder what he's talking about? I expect I'll have another injection.' After about 30 minutes a nurse appeared and said, 'I've come to wash your hair' – it felt wonderful. Half an hour later another nurse appeared with curlers, then the next nurse came along, took the curlers out and put some makeup on me. I felt absolutely fantastic – no one could have done anything better for me at that moment. Later on in the day the registrar appeared again, and I never really said thank you to him because I was so surprised that anyone could do this. It was 40 years ago that this happened, I'd like to say thank you to him and to the three nurses that also helped me.

Jacqueline, Warwickshire

After a very messy divorce in 1994 I was left on my own with three very young children, one of whom was a newborn baby; we were about to be made homeless and we didn't have anywhere to go. I didn't know what to do, and so once my son was at school, I took to going to the Wandsworth Housing Office and sitting there with my baby and four-year-old daughter hoping that something would come in. The girls there, who tried their very best to find something for us, kept saying I was wasting my time. But I was sitting there one day and a man in his 50s walked over. He sat down and asked me to tell him my story. He said he thought I had every legal right to stay in the house I was living in and that he would try and help me out. He went away and came back and said that he'd ordered a taxi for us to go to a specialist solicitor and he paid for the taxi. The solicitors got me legal aid and other help and we kept our home. I went back to the Wandsworth Housing Office later to try and find this man and say thank you to him, but surprisingly no one knew who he was, and they didn't think he worked there! Ever since then I have always thought of him as my guardian angel.

Jane, Cornwall

✳ ✳ ✳ ✳ ✳ ✳ ✳ ✳ ✳ ✳ ✳ ✳ ✳ ✳ ✳ ✳ ✳ ✳ ✳ ✳

Back in March 2008 I took it into my head that this
was going to be the weekend to walk Hadrian's Wall.
The idea was to walk it, west to east, accompanied only
by my Collie dog, Summer. Day one was absolutely
fine, but as I got into the walk on day two the novelty
had worn off a bit. An old chap who was eating a bar of
chocolate fell into step alongside me and we started a
conversation. As I told him of my plan to complete the
walk in four days he looked at me earnestly, folded the
wrapper over the remaining half of his chocolate bar,
pressed it into the palm of my hand, and said 'Take this
my dear, your need is going to be greater than mine'.
By day four, after many adventures, including a really
uncomfortable night in a rat-infested barn, and still a
few miles short of Newcastle, the dog and I collapsed
into a bird hide utterly exhausted, dishevelled and
hungry to the core. We were in a really bad way and
I thought, 'This is it, we can't go on any more.' But
then, all of a sudden, I remembered the chocolate. I
rummaged deep in my backpack, found it, and I just
gobbled that chocolate down – every last delicious
crumb. I walked purposefully out of the bird hide with
my head held high and tears streaming down my cheeks
with gratitude for that sweet gentleman's foresight. We
triumphantly reached Wallsend later that day. If I hadn't
had that chocolate I would never have finished that walk.
Thank you.

Andrea, Oxfordshire

I would like to thank a group of people in society who are largely unseen and unacknowledged and yet who have had an incalculable effect on the life of the nation – namely university accommodation officers. Their seemingly random allocation of rooms to the annual armies of freshers have shaped countless lives and friendships. In 1979 my own life was changed forever by the person who allocated rooms in my hall at Warwick University. I became friends with a girl called Claire on my corridor, and scattered around her were people who have had an enormous impact on my life ever since. Among them was Jenny, whom I married and have spent the last 30 years with, and Andy who became godfather to our two sons. Thank you.

David, Leeds

My husband and I went up to the Olympic stadium in London during the Games, just to soak up some of the atmosphere, despite the fact we had no tickets. We arrived, and were standing behind the barriers gazing at the stadium, when a young man came up behind us and asked us if we had come to see the Games. We explained we had no tickets but just wanted to experience the feel of the event. He and his friend, who were both working for the Games, offered us their guest tickets for the day and suddenly we were walking into the grounds having just been onlookers! A massive thank you to Steven Frost and Andrea Cowper for that incredibly generous gift to us – we will never forget your names!

Deirdre, Surrey

Following a motorcycle accident, I was discharged from hospital in Wiltshire on Christmas Eve, and tried to make my way home to Lancashire by train. I had only got as far as Birmingham by midnight when all the trains stopped. Stranded and feeling ill, I was helped by a stranger – I believe he worked on oil rigs – who found me a place to stay. I went in and never saw him again. Thank you.

Andrew, Dumfries and Galloway

A few years ago, while on holiday in Portugal with my fiancé Julian, son John and his girlfriend, we booked two taxis – one for my son's onward journey to Spain and my own, with Julian, to the airport for the return flight to the UK. The first taxi arrived on time and my son and his girlfriend left for Spain, leaving us to wait for the second taxi. We waited and waited until we became worried that we would miss our flight home. We walked over to the nearest town with our suitcases in very hot weather. Julian went off to find a taxi in the town whilst I stayed by the roundabout with the suitcases. Time went by, and becoming increasingly anxious, I decided to send up a prayer. Within minutes an open-topped jeep hurtled around the roundabout and screeched to a halt in front of me. 'Are you okay?' enquired the driver. 'No, I'm not', I replied, near to tears, and explained our sorry situation. The driver told me to get in and offered to go and find Julian. As we drove off I suddenly saw Julian out of the corner of my eye; he was amazed to see me perched on the jeep! The driver and his wife took us to the airport, and would not accept any recompense. After depositing our bags, we joined the queue, waved goodbye to them and rejoiced in the answer to our prayer. I would like to say a grateful thanks to our knights in shining armour for ensuring we caught our plane.

Wendy, Hertfordshire

Back in around 2003 I was waiting on Waverley Bridge in Edinburgh for a night bus back home. I got talking to a man beside me who was concerned for my safety; he felt that I shouldn't be waiting and that I should get a taxi home. I said I was fine and that I didn't have the money for a taxi. We carried on talking and he was the last person to get on his own bus and, as he got on, he put £10 into my hand. I didn't realise what it was until the bus had pulled away and I didn't get the chance to say thank you. It did mean that I was able to get a taxi home, and at that point the bus was very late, so I was really pleased to be able to do that. I want to say thank you, as it had such a positive impact on me, and it is something I would like to replicate for someone else.

Aine, Edinburgh

As a small boy in Belfast in 1950–51, during rationing and post-war privation, I had just started primary school. One day we lined up in the hall, and at the front were boxes of what turned out to be apples, which were a gift from people in British Columbia, Canada. We were each given two of the biggest, reddest apples I had ever seen. I hope the Canadians were thanked by somebody, but ever since then I've been moved when thinking about those kind people, who offered something to children they didn't know on the other side of the Atlantic. I would like to thank them, albeit many years later.

Brian, Belfast

When I was 19, I was coming back from Shetland on the overnight ferry and had a day to kill in Aberdeen. Two old ladies came over and asked if I minded if they joined me. We got talking and they said 'We're going off to lunch now, why don't you come with us?' They took me to a bistro, insisted I had a decent meal, took me round some shops and then took me to the station. They said 'We've got grandchildren and we'd like to think that if they get stranded in a strange city somewhere that someone will look after them.' They were two lovely ladies and if I ever met up with them again I'd like to say, 'Come on, let's go for lunch, I'm paying.'

Anita, East Sussex

I was in London and I hailed a cab. I got in, and immediately after starting off, the cab driver noted where I was going, the RAF Club, and began a conversation about military aeroplanes – he was particularly keen on the de Havilland Mosquito. By the time we got to the RAF Club, I got out of the cab ready to pay him, but he refused the offer and drove off. I think he made the connection between my age and my destination and realised I was an ex-serviceman. His gesture was very kind, and much appreciated.

Derek, West Sussex

— — — — — — — — — — — — — — — — — —

A friend and I were going to the theatre in Norwich and we had to find somewhere to park. Eventually we managed to find a space, and just as I was going into it, this man came rushing through at great speed and nipped into the space first. I was extremely cross but finally we found somewhere else to park, went off to the theatre and had a really nice time. When we came back, on my windscreen was a note saying, 'Sorry I stole your parking space, I don't feel good about it and it's not like me, but I was late and desperate. Hope it didn't spoil your evening too much.' With it was an enormous box of chocolates, which was amazing, and we ate all the chocolates on the way home.

Rosie, Norfolk

In 1965 I was a 16-year-old lad in Sierra Leone. My brother, who was in England, had sent for me to come and join him so I had to apply for a passport. When I went to collect it, a colonial officer asked me a few questions about where I would be studying, and who would be responsible for me in the UK, and then he said, 'When are you travelling?' I said I didn't know because I needed another £10 to make up the full fare. So he took out his wallet, got out a £10 note and gave it to me, and wished me luck. He's probably not around now but because of that £10 I was able to become the person that I am now. I have never forgotten him.

Arnold, Kent

I was on a bus from Rectory Farm to Northampton in 1981 and my purse was stolen. At the time I was a teenager who had left home; the purse contained all my money for the next two weeks and I had no other source of income. The bus driver helped me search for my purse, and when we couldn't find it he gave me £10 out of his own wallet, which was an awful lot of money then. I never knew the bus driver's name. I never properly thanked him at the time as I was so distraught, and I couldn't believe anybody could be so generous and so kind. I think of him often. He has no idea what a hole he got me out of and presumably he would have gone without himself.

Louise, Northamptonshire

I'd like to thank my beloved younger brother who died in Paris in 1998, and left me a sum of money in his will that I was able to use as a deposit to buy a small house in Kingston. Without his generous legacy I would not have been able to do this, and for many years I was both grateful and incredibly sad that it was his death that enabled me and my two girls to gain the security of owning our own home.

Elena, Greater London

I would like to thank a lovely lady called Ann Bantoft who, in the summer of 1969, gave me – a 20-year-old, penniless paratrooper, stationed in Malta and hitchhiking back to England – a lift from Florence in Italy all the way back home to the Dartford Tunnel. She paid for my lodgings, bought me food and drink (even though her funds were limited). I did send her a big bunch of flowers but I have since lost contact with her due to my travels. She was a brave and generous lady.

Eddie, Norfolk

In October 1999 we got the telephone call that every parent dreads: while riding his motorbike in St Lucia, our son Dominic had been hit by a drunk driver. The injuries to his legs were so severe that he had been airlifted to La Meynard, the main hospital in Fort de France, Martinique. I immediately flew to Paris and then to Martinique to be with him. One of the other patients in his room was an elderly local man who had just had a replacement hip. His family would visit him daily and we became 'nodding' acquaintances because of the language barrier between English and French. It was a tradition to take food into the hospital to supplement the offerings from the hospital kitchens. Dominic stayed in the hospital for about two weeks, when the decision was made to transfer him to the rehabilitation hospital at Le Carbet, some 64km (40 miles) away. While travelling between St Lucia and Martinique I was unlucky enough to be caught up in the aftermath of Hurricane Lenny. I finally made it through the torrential rain to Le Carbet and was glad to see that Dom had been successfully transferred. He told me I had just missed the French family from La Meynard who had braved the hurricane wind and rain to bring him some food. We never knew their names and never will but their kindness and generosity will stay in our memories forever.

Lou, Hertfordshire

In 1969, when I was a young Irishman, I worked as a barman in Kings Cross, London. Due to unforeseen circumstances I left my employment and soon found myself homeless. While having a pint in my old pub one evening, a regular customer, a Jamaican called Brady, asked me how I was coping, and I told him I wasn't. He gave me £20 and told me to pay it back when I could afford to. I found a flat and a job in another area thanks to Brady's kindness. At the time, £20 was a lot of money, especially for someone on a low wage. I tried several times to find him but never saw Brady again.

Brian, County Louth, Ireland

I was stuck at Istanbul airport waiting to fly home after spending the summer vacation working on an archaeological dig in Turkey. But the passport control official wouldn't let me through and consequently I missed the plane. Fortunately, I was able to get help from a kind chap who could speak Turkish and he gave me a lift back to Istanbul, and eventually I was able to go to the British Embassy and get sorted out. I've always remembered the kindness of that guy who helped me out in the middle of the night when I was stranded with no money and no one to talk to.

Robert, Leicester

When the mayors of London decided to launch a New York-style New Year's Day parade, those of us who worked for the London Borough of Havering had to take part: the theme for our float was 'Romford, historic market town'. I was appropriately dressed as a peasant so I dumped my coat and bag in the support bus, and I walked behind the float to the end of the route, which was just outside Buckingham Palace. You are not allowed to stop there, but the support bus slowed down and everybody ran and got in – apart from me. Gradually the bus began to speed up. I was running, waving and shouting, but they didn't notice and I was left behind. It was a bank holiday and icy cold; I had no coat and no money. In the end I thought I would just go and throw myself on the mercy of London Underground. I said to them, 'I've got no money and I need to get home.' And that's when the magic happened. In the queue someone said, 'I'll buy you a ticket, where do you want to go?' I would so like to say thank you to that gentleman. He was my angel of the New Year.

Chris, Greater London

When I was 17 my expatriate parents decided, for several reasons, to send me on my own by sea to Britain from India. During the voyage I developed measles and was quite ill. When I got to the docks, where I was supposed to be met by some people, they were not there. I don't know how my luggage and I ended up at Liverpool station, but that's where I found myself, not knowing what to do. A middle-aged porter came up and asked if I needed help, and this wonderful man found the train I needed to catch to get to Largs in Scotland, and installed my luggage and me in a carriage. He must have also bought a ticket for me; I didn't think of that at the time. I do so hope that I felt well enough to thank him for his care and generosity at the time. I will never forget him.

Liz, Greater London

In July 2002 my sister-in-law Joy died suddenly and unexpectedly. The following day, my husband and his brother drove from Surrey to Bournemouth, to break the news to their elderly father that his youngest child had died. Meanwhile, their sister and I drove to Wiltshire to spend the day with our bereaved brother-in-law and his devastated children. Our shock and sorrow lay heavily on us as we drove home, and we commented that we would love to find an old-fashioned tea shop – rather than a busy café with Formica-topped tables – where we could break the journey. In the next village we spotted just such a tea shop and parked the car, only to find a 'closed' sign on the door. Our hearts sank, but the lady inside noticed us, opened the door and said, 'You look like ladies who need a cup of tea', and sat us down while she served us. I have never forgotten her kindness and have often told others about it.

Jennifer, Sheffield

During the winter of 1982 at about one o'clock in the morning, after a late rehearsal with my band, I was walking home from Kingston to Fulham. It was raining heavily and I was about halfway up Kingston Hill. A car pulled up, a Robin Reliant, and a nice Rastafarian chap leaned out and said 'Do you want a lift?' I jumped in the car thanking him very much – I was absolutely soaking wet. He clearly had a brilliant sense of humour because the whole of the inside of his car was covered with leopard-skin fun fur and it had the first real sound system I had ever seen. He drove me not just towards where I was going, but literally to my front door so I didn't have to go out into the rain again, and disappeared off into the night. I have given people lifts many times since with his kindness in the back of my mind.

Leon

In my early 20s I set out alone to walk the Coast to Coast path, completely ill-equipped and inexperienced, with no pre-booked accommodation. I set out on a bank holiday weekend and everywhere was full. In a pub on the first evening, two guys who were travelling with their children heard me asking about a room, and invited me to camp with them. Based on the behaviour of their children, I took the risk and accepted. They, Simon and Garth, were fantastic, welcomed me into the warmth of their very special parent/child holiday, and even drove me back to the pub to continue my walk in the morning. Their kindness restored my faith in the world, and helped me stick with my plan and finish the trip. That walk was a key life experience, and I have always wanted to let them know that I made it, and to say thank you.

Penny, East Sussex

I married an American and I came back to Oxford to retire. One day I went to visit my solicitor in London. I hadn't had breakfast or lunch and when I got to the Tube station I thought I'd better get some sort of bite to eat. At the entrance there was a very nice-looking young lady and I asked her if she knew where I could buy a candy bar. She pointed across the park and said there was a shop there; I told her it was too far and I would just wait until I got home. I sat on a bench and waited for the train and then the young lady appeared with a whole box of chocolates! She walked away and I got on the train, but I really would like to thank her in person.

Jane, Oxfordshire

My husband Mike and I were honeymooning in Budapest in October 1985. We didn't have a lot of money, but we decided to treat ourselves to dinner at the hotel. We were queuing up for a table and ahead of us were two couples, also British. The head waiter came across and said there was a table for six available. They turned around and asked if we would like to join them. The first thing that happened was that they ordered a bottle of champagne and then they started to order dinner. One of the gentlemen asked me if I would like to share a chateaubriand with him, so Mike and I had a whispered conversation, and decided we could survive on bread and water for the rest of the week if we needed to. We steeled ourselves for the arrival of the bill and when we tried to offer to pay the other two couples would hear nothing of it. We have always wanted to say thank you – we still dine out on that story!

Stella, Lincolnshire

In 1991, when my son was on his gap year, he had run out of money and was hungry having not eaten for three days and, without money for the ferry, he was stranded in Athens. He knew no one and didn't know who to turn to. He went to the British Embassy to ask if they could help, but they told him to book into a hotel and ring home to arrange for some money to be sent. Without the means to do that, and feeling very dejected, he left the embassy, but the security guard saw his worried face, and when my son had told him the story, he gave him the money. As the anxious mother of a 19-year-old I'd like to say a big thank you to the security guard, wherever he is now.

Juliet, Gloucestershire

In 1985, when I was 27, I was offered the opportunity to DJ in Cairo. Two weeks into my contract I got my first pay cheque, and found they had paid me in Egyptian pounds rather than English pounds (a tenth of the value), and decided not to continue working. Over breakfast one morning I explained that I couldn't get home without asking for money from my parents. A young lady in the group, who was a dancer at a large casino, lent me the money and gave me a scrap of paper saying 'Please give the money to my parents when you can.' I came home but I lost the piece of paper with her parents' name and address. I would like to say how grateful I am these many years later.

Martyn, West Sussex

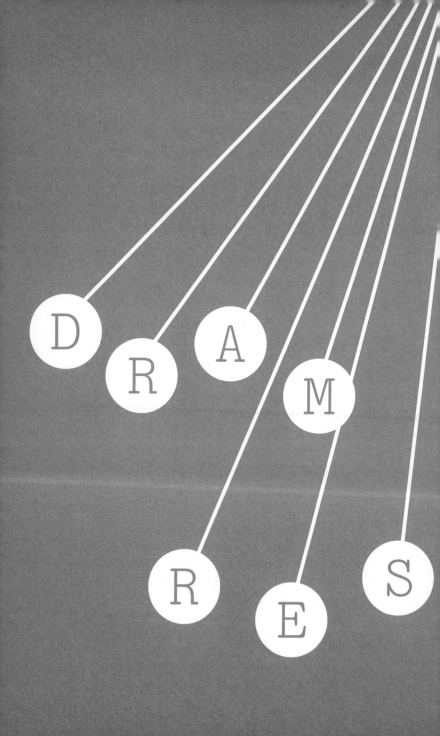

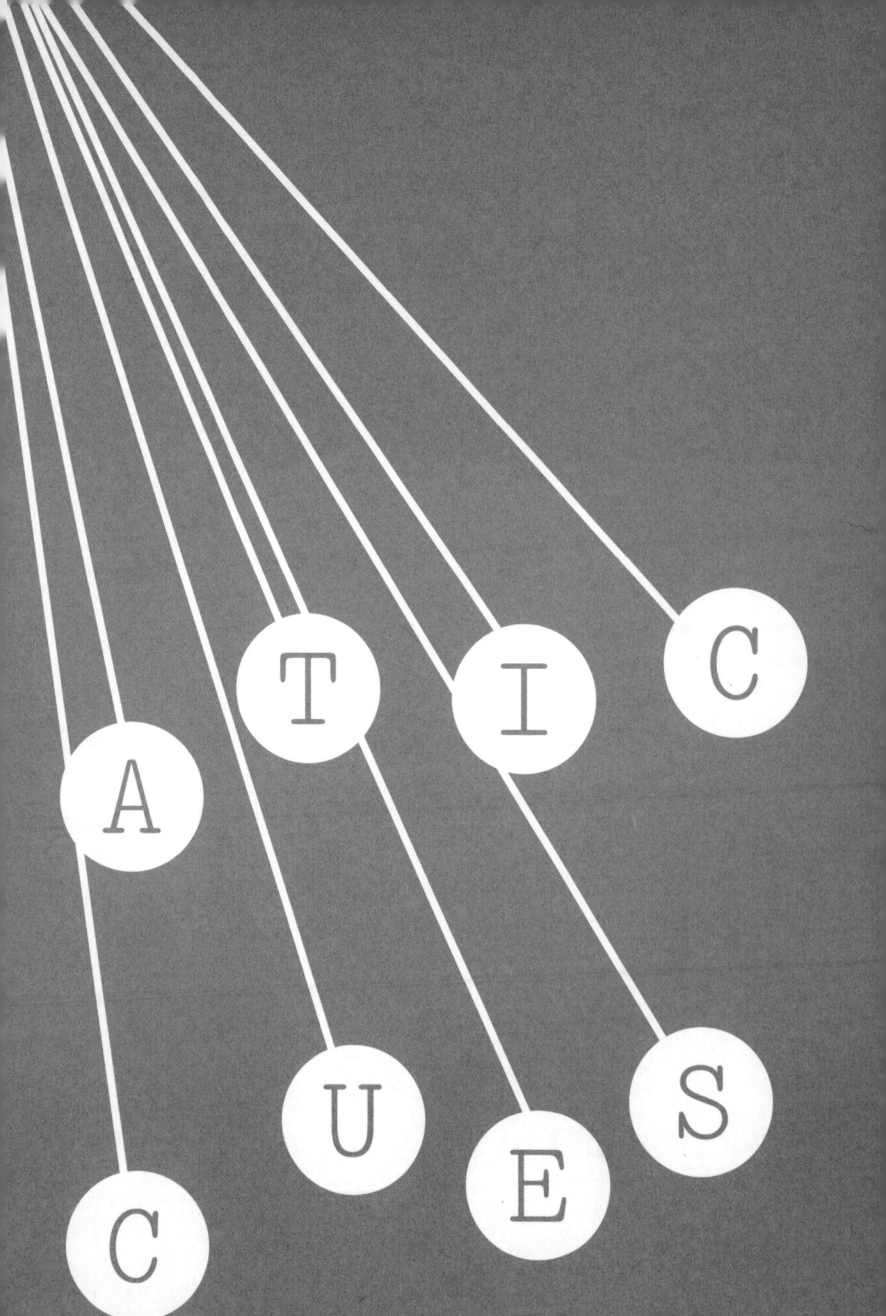
A T I C
C U E S

'As we express our gratitude, we must never forget that the highest appreciation is not to utter words, but to live by them.'

JOHN F. KENNEDY

It is the moment we all dread, when ourselves or a loved one is in imminent danger and we are helpless. It is at times like this that the human spirit both baffles and amazes, when people we do not know put themselves at risk for others without a moment's thought. In this collection of stories people are rescued at sea and from lakes, falling from building and trains, and even pulled from burning cars. It is thanks to their rescuers that these contributors have lived to tell their tales, and to say thank you.

In May 2012, I was flying my paraglider along the cliff at Eype in Dorset, when one side of it collapsed and I hit the cliff with my right hip. The wing caught on something on the cliff top and two coastal path walkers, with great presence of mind, sat on it. I was unaware of this as I was 20ft (6m) from the top and in great pain, having dislocated my hip. I pulled out my phone and dialled 999 only to see the message 'No network coverage'. Two friends were flying with me and I knew they would call the emergency services. The Portland Coastguard helicopter was there in 25 minutes and took me to Dorchester Hospital. I wrote to the Fire Service and Portland Coastguard to thank them but I never found out who the two walkers were. I should like to say a very big thank you to them for stopping me sliding down to the beach 170ft (52m) below. I'd also like to repeat my thanks to Dorset Fire Service and the Portland Coastguard. As my daughter said: 'Bit of a daft way to get a new hip!'

Richard, Somerset

I'd like to thank the person who grabbed me as I fell out of a train. This happened in the summer of 1949, the week before my second birthday. I was standing on tiptoe trying to look out of the window, playing with the catch, when the door flew open. I'm told I was well into free fall before the man sitting opposite my father reached out and grabbed me and brought me back, for which I am extraordinarily grateful. It was a wonderful thing to do and it was quick thinking – it must have been the matter of a second or so. But if anyone recognises himself, thank you very much.

Robin, Kent

I was on holiday with my parents near Bournemouth in 1957 when I was nine years old. I would like to say a very belated thank you to the young man who pulled me out of the sea – unconscious – and in doing so saved my life. I woke up on the tarmac on the seafront undergoing artificial respiration. If my memory serves me right, he lived in Romford and my father thanked him by sending him a premium bond. I've often wondered how much it was for – I do hope it proved lucky and he won some money! Thank you for saving my life.

Sue, Cornwall

In 1983 I was walking through Kingston Market pushing my two-year-old daughter in a pushchair. All of a sudden she started to choke and turn blue. It happened so rapidly. She couldn't breathe; I had no idea what was wrong or what to do. I just stood and screamed for help. I felt terrified and helpless. Suddenly a complete stranger, a man, lifted her out of her chair, held her upside-down and thumped her in the centre of her upper back. A sweet that had lodged in her throat shot out and in seconds she was back in her chair and breathing normally. I thanked him but not nearly enough. I was so overwhelmed that she was safe. He was gone as quickly as he appeared. I have no doubt he saved her life. Thank you. Oh, thank you!

Anne, Surrey

I'd like to thank two strangers who saved my life in the 1950s as an 18-month-old child. I was playing on the balcony of a third-floor council block apartment when I dropped a favourite toy. As I climbed up to get it I slipped over the side but managed to hang on to a railing. Two men were working on the building site opposite, they heard me scream, looked across and saw me dangling. They raced over, stood below me and crossed their arms in a fireman's catch and, as I tumbled, they broke my fall and saved my life. I'd like to say thank you, albeit 50-odd years later.

Robert, Glasgow

In 1990, we were visiting my wife's sister in Perth with our four-year-old son, Kieran. The three of us were on the beach and my wife, Helen, went for a swim while I looked after Kieran. Whilst swimming, she waved at us. We waved back. She kept waving; so we did too. I suddenly realised she was waving for help! I ran down the beach shouting to a nearby couple to look after Kieran. As I neared the water's edge, a young 'surfie' was walking along. I grabbed his arm and pointed to Helen in distress and asked him to help. We both dived in and swam out to her – she was caught in the undertow. We got to her okay but then had great trouble swimming back. When we eventually reached the beach, exhausted and panting for breath, we were only able to gasp a thank you to the guy before he sauntered off as though it were an everyday event for him. He risked his life to save Helen and I believe he saved me too as I don't think I could have done it on my own. We profusely thanked the couple that looked after Kieran but never had the chance to thank the 'surfie' guy. I hope this reaches him these 23 years later.

John, Surrey

I was in Hong Kong in my car in June 1966. We had had over 48 hours of brutal, non-stop rain. I crawled up Victoria Peak in low gear but just as my flat appeared ahead, a woman stood in front of my car miming that I should stop. She pointed to the road surface: it looked like bubbling pastry and she signed that I shouldn't go on further. I smiled, nodded my thanks, reversed my car down the hill and tucked it into a sedan chair path – these follow the lie of the land and survive bad weather well. In fact the road had become a giant landslide. We were cut off for weeks until a bridge could be built to reconnect us to the town and we had to have our food delivered by helicopter. There is no way I can ever thank that wonderful woman but I am forever grateful.

Frances, Devon

I was travelling with my boyfriend from Bolivia to the Brazilian border. We were on a little rural bus in the jungle and some armed military-looking men came on board and motioned for me to get off the bus. As my boyfriend got up they pushed him back into his seat and they made me go into a little hut. There were four of them standing there in their uniforms speaking in Portuguese. I tried to explain that I didn't speak Portuguese but they shouted more and more and then they got their guns out. It became apparent that they wanted me to strip. I remember having a strange, out-of-body experience that I was looking down on myself, watching as I stripped off my clothes. Suddenly, a Portuguese lady, a little bit older than me, walked in, pushed past these men, put herself in front of me and tried to cover me while shouting back at the men. Eventually I could see that somehow they had come to an agreement that they would let us go. We walked out and got back on the bus; she sat at the front, I went to the back and the bus carried on. Over that night we spent on the bus I realised what probably would have happened to me, and I realised that this woman had put herself in front of these men to save a complete stranger. When the bus finally arrived in Brazil, I pushed my way to the front to find the lady, but she had gone. She was a true guardian angel and I often think of her and how she saved my life.

Natalia

I want to say thank you to the American man who saved my three-year-old daughter's life as he pulled her out of a hidden pond at Chelsea Physic Garden 11 years ago. I was chasing after my toddler, aged two, and didn't see my daughter fall in the pond. I was so shocked I never thanked him as I rushed off to get her dry in the toilets. I think of him often and know she wouldn't be alive today without his swift action. Thank you.

Catherine, London

When I was 17 I took my first car to England from Jersey to see my girlfriend. One night, on the A34 near Solihull, I overtook a car at the top of a hill and collided head-on with another. My car had its fuel tank in the front and burst into flames with me stuck inside it. I was partially conscious, my foot was stuck between the pedals and the doors were jammed. The driver of the other car pulled me through the passenger window and saved me. I never got to thank him, though I tried to contact him through the Warwickshire Police Force years later.

Gerard, Jersey

This story goes right back to 1973 and I would love to thank a chap who rescued my daughter on the beach at Thorpeness in Suffolk. She was playing with a beach ball and the next thing I knew she was being swept out to sea. I was a very poor swimmer and she could hardly swim either. There was a man on the beach who saw what was happening and he rescued her. I then got back to the shore myself and before I could say thank you properly he'd gone. The guy that rescued her is a hero because I think we would both have sunk.

Jeremy, Somerset

In the summer of 1986 I was taking my two small boys to the Natural History Museum to see the dinosaurs. We had left early so that we would have a full day and consequently we arrived at Liverpool Street Station at 8.45am – right in the middle of the rush hour. On reflection, it was probably not such a good idea to travel with a five-year-old and an 18-month-old at this time of day, but holding hands with one and with the other in the pushchair, we were fine. We were on the platform waiting for the Tube train that would take us to South Kensington; it was very crowded, with people jostling for position. When the train pulled in the doors opened and my elder child got on and I turned to pick up the little one in the pushchair. As I did so the doors closed, leaving me with one child on the outside and the other one on his own inside the train. It happened that quickly! I looked for buttons on the door and searched desperately for a guard, but the platform was so crowded, it was just a sea of people. I banged on the door of the train and a gentleman who had been sitting reading his newspaper assessed the situation and calmly got up, pulled the communication cord, and then sat down again and continued to read his paper. The doors opened and I was able to give my son a big, frantic, panicky hug and get on the train. I have never been so relieved! In the short time he was on the train my mind raced through everything that could have happened to him and even now when I think of it my stomach churns. So thank you to the man who pulled the handle. I will always be grateful to you.

Judi, Essex

Thirty years ago, my youngest daughter and her friend were cut off by the tide at Bonchurch, Isle of Wight. Somebody on the cliff saw them and alerted the coastguard, an RAF helicopter picked them up, and then landed on Sandown beach. Thank you to the person who called the coastguard.

Pam, Isle of Wight

I was on holiday in Albufeira in Portugal in the 1970s with my teenage son. We booked with two new friends to go on a boat trip organised by the hotel. We were to go to a nearby cove that was only accessible by small boats. Our large boat had to anchor while we had the choice either to swim the fairly long distance or wait for the smaller boats. The sea was rough, but my son and our friend swam off, leaving his wife and me to wait. I started to feel very seasick, so we bravely decided to jump off and swim. I very soon got into difficulties in the choppy sea. I knew I wasn't going to be able to make it and I panicked. My son and our friend spotted us from the beach and realised I was in trouble. An American man on the beach then joined our friend and they swam out and rescued me. I would like to say a late but enormous thank you to that stranger who helped rescue a very frightened lady.

Janet, Dorset

In the late 1950s, when I was three or four years old, my father worked for the Post Office. At that time the PO had offices at Bletchley Park and that is where my father was based. One weekend my parents and some friends decided to have a game of tennis on their courts. My sister, who was seven or eight, and I were left to feed the ducks on the lake at the front of the main building. Unfortunately, I fell into the lake, which could not be seen from the tennis courts. All I know is that a young man, who was wearing a yellow jumper, pulled me out of the lake while my sister was running to get my parents. In the panic and confusion the man in the yellow jumper left the lake before my mother and father had time to thank him. I would like to take this opportunity to say thank you; if he is still around he would probably at least 80 by now.

Diane, Buckinghamshire

When I was on a skiing holiday in Les Arcs in France, I was about to go down a flight of metal stairs, when I tripped on the top step. I went flying through the air and it went through my mind that 'This was it!' Then a very nice Frenchman caught me in mid-air. I would just like to say thank you because I think he saved my life.

Sylvia, Kinross-shire

On Wednesdays we look after our grandson, Arlo. One Wednesday in December 2012, we wrapped up warmly and went to Hyde Park in London, with a plan to walk around the Serpentine. On the north shore of the lake I was pushing the buggy while my husband, Peter, and Arlo were walking along behind. I parked the buggy but failed to put the brake on. It went straight into the lake and started to sink, with gloves, shopping and nappy-changing bag floating gently away. Suddenly a couple in running gear arrived on the scene and offered assistance. In a trice, the handsome young man had stripped down to his underpants and launched out into the freezing water. He gallantly retrieved everything while we shouted thanks and encouragement, but he humbly said the main thing was that Arlo hadn't been in the buggy. Lots of people swim in the Serpentine in December, but they choose to and they come prepared. What a hero!

Florence, London

In the summer of 2010 I was swimming on the beach at Bude in Cornwall with some friends. It was about six o'clock in the evening and the lifeguards had left for the day. After a few minutes I realised I was much further out than was safe for me, as I'm not a strong swimmer, and I had got caught in some kind of current. The more I tried to swim back the further I seemed to go. My head went under the waves a few times and I thought I was going to drown. I stuck my arm in the air and screamed for help and shortly afterwards I was rescued by two young surfers with their boards. It took them about 10 minutes to get me in. I was exhausted and in shock and I never had the chance to apologise for my stupidity and to thank them properly. I was 47 at the time and had been through a lot of problems with addiction and depression; I had actually spent quite a few of the preceding years wanting to die. Now I'm 51, and am teaching again, and have found a new career/passion in acting. I always feel humbled when I remember that those young men, at least half my age, did something for me that I couldn't do for myself – they helped teach me the value of life.

Declan, London

The collapsed ceiling at the Apollo Theatre in December 2013 reminded me of a thank you I never offered when, aged two or so, the ceiling of my bedroom descended without warning. I was saved from injury by the arms, shoulders and head of a truly wonderful person called Emmy Hamblin, who has now probably passed on, who looked after me when I was a baby. I'd love to hear from her daughter and my surrogate sister Anne – then I could thank Auntie through her. She is often in my thoughts.

Jonathan, Cornwall

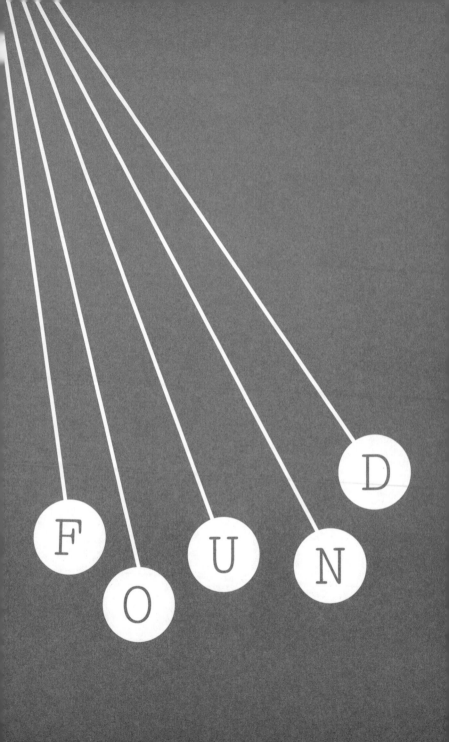

'Thank you is the best prayer that anyone could say. I say that one a lot. Thank you expresses extreme gratitude, humility, understanding.'

ALICE WALKER

Our possessions are important
to us for different reasons,
and an item does not have to
be worth a lot to mean a great
deal. In this collection of
stories a wide variety of
items are returned to their
grateful owners by strangers
who expect nothing in return:
the only copy of a student's
dissertation that fell off the
roof of a car in Edinburgh;
a violin that was left on a
bus in the United States; a
lost child on a crowded summer
beach; and a favourite pair
of gloves lost in a car park.
Fortunately all these things
were reunited with their owners,
who would like to take this
opportunity to say thank you.

I had just started my three-year-old daughter Elinor with a new childminder, Gwen. Gwen had her own little boy, Michael, four, and Gwen's older child needed to be picked up from school, so she took her husband a cup of tea and said 'I've left Ellie and Michael downstairs watching a video, go and look after them.' A short time later he went downstairs to find the front door open – and no children. He assumed they had followed Gwen to the school but when he got there of course they hadn't. What the children told us later was that the video finished and so they went to the video shop to get another one. To get to the video shop, they had to cross a really busy main road onto a roundabout, and cross a road on the other side. They got themselves into the video shop but, as Elinor said, 'We didn't have any money!' It was at this point that a wonderful woman, watching from her office, had seen what was happening and grabbed them as they came out. She took them into the local GP surgery, where Michael was recognised, and us frantic parents were contacted. Thank you to that lady, we never knew who you were, but we are always in your debt.

Helen, London

I would like to thank a gentleman whom I met in Brussels in the early 1960s. I was sitting in the sun outside a café and we fell into conversation. He asked me if I'd been to see the sights outside Brussels, and when I said I hadn't he offered to drive me out there to have a look. We had a little drive around, he dropped me off at the station, and said goodbye. I later realised I'd left a small clutch bag in his car. I was very surprised a few days later, after I had got back, when a parcel arrived – it was my clutch bag coming back safely to me. He certainly was a gentleman and I've never forgotten that very nice favour and my day in Brussels.

Ann, Surrey

I was out shopping in Beverley, Yorkshire, and I loaded up the car and I think I must have dropped my purse in a dark part of the Marks & Spencer car park. I drove home and realised I'd lost my purse – I had that horrible feeling of knowing that all my cards and everything else were lost. By the time I got back the shop was closing, but they opened up because they actually had my purse – some really lovely person had picked it up in the car park and handed it in. My horrible feeling was replaced by a renewal of my faith in mankind.

Jane, East Yorkshire

My disabled brother Stuart lost his gold wristwatch at Otley bus station and was very upset about it. His right hand and arm are paralysed and he carries his watch in his pocket as he can only use his left arm. A few weeks later, Stuart was once again waiting at the bus station when he was approached by a gentleman and his wife who explained that the last time they had seen him they noticed he was looking for something. The man had found his watch and kept it in his pocket until he saw Stuart again. As you can imagine, Stuart was so happy and thrilled that he had got his watch back and that this gentleman was so honest and kind. I was so pleased for him and would like to pass on a great big thank you to this person for his kindness and honesty.

Wendy, West Yorkshire

During the 1990s I was in Hamburg, Germany, to give a lecture. I took the train to the university where I was speaking, and as I got off I thought I saw someone waving. I thought nothing of it, but when I arrived at the university I realised I had lost the bag in which I was carrying my lecture slides, clean shirt, tie and money. I hurried to the shops to buy a new shirt and tie, quickly rethought my lecture, changed and then rushed into the hall to give my lecture – it wasn't too bad! Afterwards, I went to my hotel and the receptionist said a taxi driver had been looking for me and had left a phone number. I called the number, and a man came to the hotel – with my bag. He said, 'My son was on your train and he saw you leave your bag behind. He knows I call at a lot of hotels and he told me to ask at every hotel until I found you.' I was so grateful and I asked the man to thank his son, and give him some money from me as a reward. He said 'No, he is a good Muslim boy, and he was just doing what he knows he should.' At the time I was Headteacher at a big multi-ethnic school near London, and the following Monday I retold the story in school assembly, with a suitable moral message at the end. It went down very well, but afterwards the Deputy Head said to me 'I bet you left that bag on the train deliberately – you'd do anything to get good subject matter for assembly!' So thank you to the boy, now a man, in Hamburg who gave me not only my bag, but also a great assembly story.

John, Yorkshire

I was travelling by shuttle bus from New York's La
Guardia Airport to Penn Station on my way to a
conference upstate, where I was to play my violin.
To my surprise we screeched to a halt outside the
familiar dome of Grand Central instead, with the driver
bellowing that we should hurry to catch the bus down
the street if we wanted to continue to Penn. I grabbed
my suitcase and started in the direction he had pointed
but, within a few steps, realised that I was missing my
violin. I turned on my heel but it was too late. The bus
sped off and my heart exploded with panic. A frantic
half hour on the dispatcher's radio followed, with every
driver returning the same sentiment: 'There is no violin
aboard this bus.' I was about to give up hope when I
heard a woman's voice crackle over the air: 'I have your
violin and I'll bring it to you.' On the other end was the
singsong voice of an operatic soprano from Memphis
who picked up my violin knowing – as only a fellow
musician could – that somebody would be missing it
terribly. When the bus pulled in she passed it to me and,
with a theatrical air kiss, disappeared into the crowded
streets of Manhattan. I think of her often when I play.
It is the best I can do, having been unable to thank her
properly at the time!

Victoria, Texas, USA

In 1994 we were driving back from a holiday in Wales with two kids in the rear seats, two dogs in the boot, and three suitcases strapped to the roof. My husband Andy suddenly shouted, 'Oh no! One of the cases has fallen off the roof!' We looked back to see a stream of our unwashed clothes flying around the inside lane of the M1. Andy pulled onto the hard shoulder and he and I got out to see if we could retrieve any of our belongings. Suddenly, all three lanes of the motorway slowed and then stopped in unison, and the occupants of the cars and lorries all got out and helped us to pick everything up! It was a surreal sight, but I am grateful for all the help those car and lorry drivers gave us, and I would like to say a huge thank you to every one of them!

Karen, Suffolk

I travelled from Leeds to London to visit my dad and sister one Saturday afternoon, and while I was on the train I checked emails and did some work on my iPad. After leaving the train at King's Cross I had a couple of other things to do in London before the long Tube ride to my sister's. When I eventually arrived, I opened my case, and realised to my horror that the iPad wasn't there. In a panic I rang the British Transport Police to report the item lost or stolen and after I put the phone down I called my husband in Leeds, absolutely disconsolate, to tell him about the loss of the iPad, which had several important pieces of work in progress stored on it that were not duplicated anywhere else. My husband listened patiently to my lament and then said, 'A bloke has just come to our door and handed your iPad to me. He was working on the train, found it under a pile of newspapers at the end of the journey, opened your emails and realised he lived near us in Leeds. He came straight to our door to return it.' I'm so sorry I wasn't there to give the man a big hug of gratitude. Thank you.

Sheena, Yorkshire

One afternoon our gorgeous but ditsy Golden Retriever, Nellie, escaped from the garden and took herself for a walk down to the main road through the village – Spetisbury in Dorset. I want to thank the unknown kind man who heroically braked and almost avoided hitting her, then left his car to follow her down a path to the river, and rang a doorbell for help in finding her. She was only bruised and is now fine. It would have been far worse without his kindness. Thank you so much.

Anna, Dorset

I want to say thank you to the honest person who found my pearl bracelet in Sainsbury's in Woolton, Liverpool, and handed it in to Customer Services. The bracelet is priceless. Just weeks before I lost it, I had given my granddaughter earrings for her eighteenth birthday made from six pearls that had been taken from the bracelet. The bracelet is to be hers, together with a matching ring, when I am no longer here. I did try to find the name of the kind person but to no avail. My thanks are profound.

Joan, Liverpool

I was driving across the New Mexican desert
and stopped at a filling station. As I re-joined the
freeway, a truck behind me was beeping its horn
and flashing its lights: I thought the driver was mad.
Half an hour later I pulled over to take a photo, and
found that I no longer had my camera or the small
travel pouch it had been in, which also contained
my passport, plane tickets and more than $1,000
in cash and travellers' cheques. I remembered I'd
put it on the car roof when filling up and had left
it there – that's what the truck driver had seen. I
drove back, with little hope. The truck driver had
stopped on the freeway when the pouch fell off
the roof, driven many miles to the next exit, driven
back to the filling station and handed in the pouch,
leaving no name or address. The whole operation
must have taken him almost an hour. Thank you.

John, North Wales

One hot summer's day in 1995 our family – parents, two teenagers and a four-year-old – descended on Holkham Beach, North Norfolk. The beach is vast and that day it was packed with people. We located a picnic spot and then in a blinding flash of panic we realised our little girl was nowhere to be seen. My older daughter stayed at base whilst my son, husband and I each went in a different direction. For what seemed like an eternity I walked around calling 'Francesca!' and stopped to ask various groups of people if they had seen a little girl in a pink skirt and plaits. Everyone promised to keep an eye out for her. Then I heard a woman's voice in the distance calling 'Helena!' – I have never been so glad that I have a slightly unusual first name. This lady and her daughter took me up to an elevated spot on the dunes – an ideal lookout post. Her friend was looking after a distraught little girl, who was at least able to give her mummy's name, while they surveyed the beach below. Francesca and I were so emotional and relieved to be reunited that I scarcely thought to thank those women, and by the time I had recovered myself they had gone, but we were both so grateful.

Helena, Nottinghamshire

Twenty-five years ago, when I was a final year student studying Archaeology at Edinburgh University, I used to drive around the city in a beaten-up old Mini Clubman. On the night in question, I had driven away from the Archaeology department leaving my nearly completed, handwritten dissertation and all my notes on the roof of the car. The work was unnamed and nowhere in sight, when I realised what had happened, and returned to the scene. Horror and misery reigned for three days as the deadline for the dissertation approached and I had no hope of getting the work done again. Miraculously on the fourth day a parcel appeared in the library addressed to me. It was all there down to the very last scribble, together with a note, 'Your guardian angel was watching you.' I tried at the time to find out who had rescued me so amazingly but I never did. Thank you.

Katie, Edinburgh

✛✛✛✛✛✛✛✛✛✛✛✛✛✛✛✛✛✛✛

Our daughter told us sadly that she'd lost a nice purse we bought her years ago: it contained money, her driving licence and credit cards. Two weeks later the purse, with all its contents intact, arrived by post at our house in Wales – the address on her driving licence. The lovely person who found and sent it didn't include their name and we would like to say thank you.

Daphne, Gwynedd

I was out shopping one weekend in Liskeard in
Cornwall and I thought 'I don't know where I left
my gloves' – they weren't in my pockets. As I
approached the car I saw something on the bonnet
and it was my gloves. Somebody had taken the
trouble to pick them up off the floor – I must have
dropped them when I got out – and put them on
the bonnet of the car for me. These gloves have
melded to my hands, they are like a pair of old
slippers, and I really would be lost without them.
I hope this person, whoever they are, has a kindness
repaid to them because they certainly deserve it.

Pauline, Cornwall

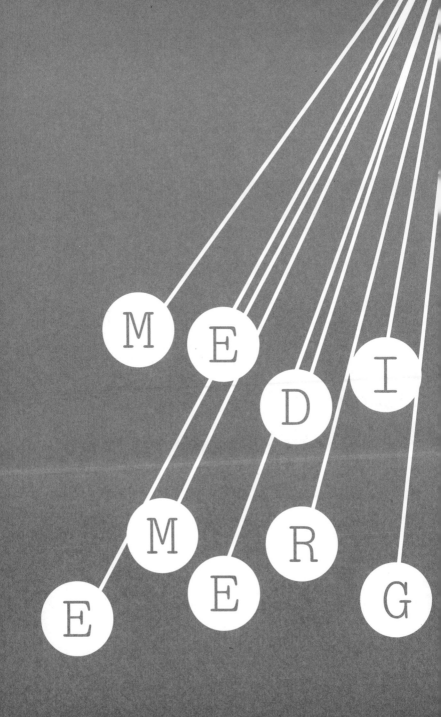

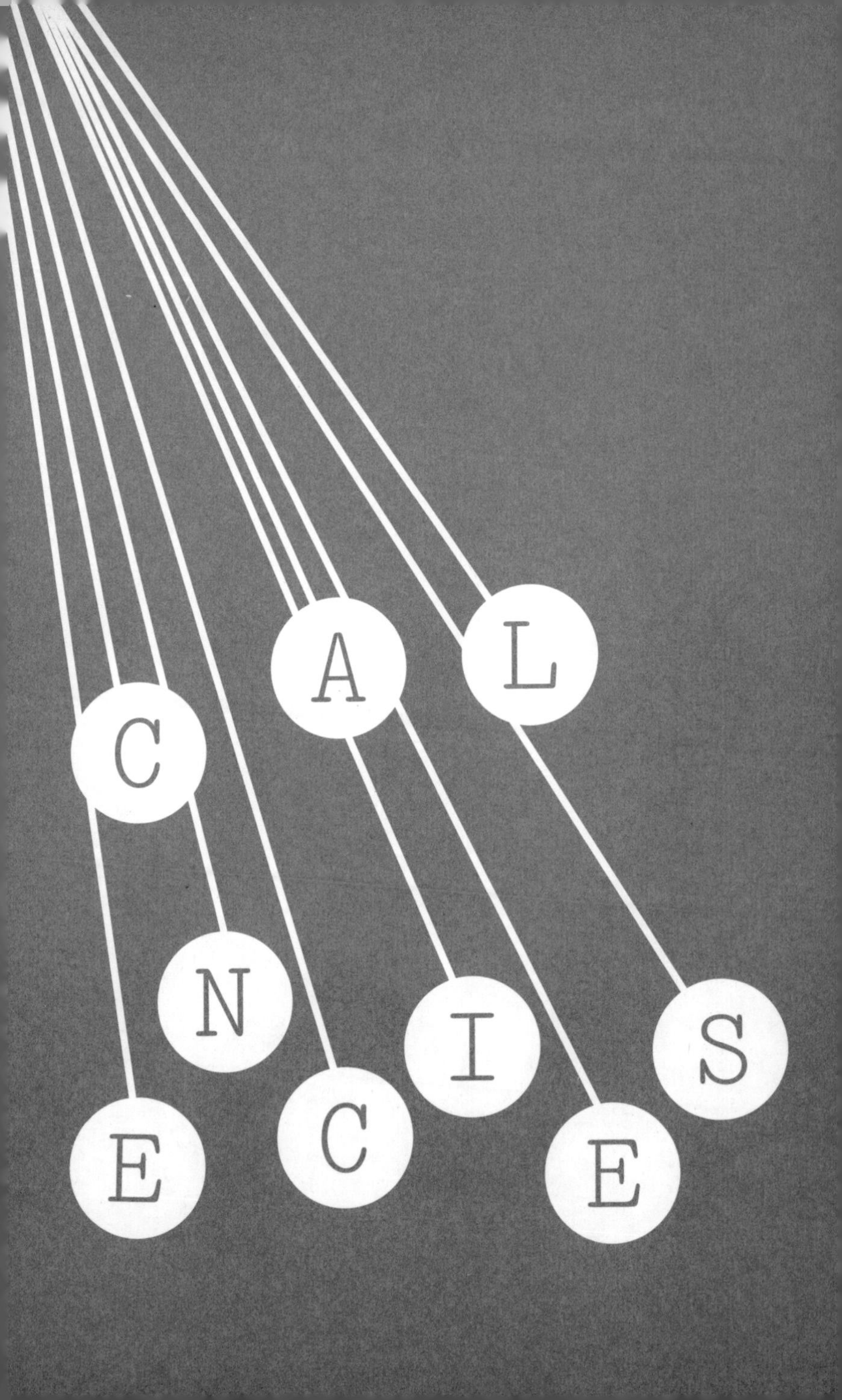
C A L
N I S
E C E

'Gratitude bestows reverence, allowing us to encounter everyday epiphanies, those transcendent moments of awe that change forever how we experience life and the world.'

JOHN MILTON

Being taken ill, or dealing
with a medical condition,
is when we are at our most
vulnerable. We are fortunate
then that there are so many
wonderful people, both inside
and outside the medical
profession, who are prepared
to help us. This collection
includes stories from a
man who was comforted by a
stranger while suffering a
brain haemorrhage, a woman
whose husband was helped after
collapsing on a Tube train, and
the man whose life-threatening
condition was detected
following a conversation with
a concerned taxi driver.

After a Michael Ball concert in Bristol I felt ill. I got into a taxi to take me to the station to catch the last train back to Exeter. By the time we got there I was too ill to get out and the driver took me to A&E without accepting a fare. He even visited me the following day and still didn't accept the money. Eventually, after over two weeks of tests, I was diagnosed with a rare aortic aneurism in the aortic arch which, had it ruptured, would have killed me. Having recovered from surgery lasting six hours, I returned home and have since seen my second son married and three grandchildren born. I might never have met them had that taxi driver not been so caring. I would so love to thank him in person.

Maggie, Devon

The day after Boxing Day in 2005, we went to
Bluewater shopping centre in Kent. Suddenly I felt
an intense pain in my head, it was spinning and I was
violently ill. Then I was aware that a lady had come
and sat next to me; she put her arms round me and she
comforted me. I was having a brain haemorrhage. She
was just there, she calmed me down; I didn't know what
was happening and I was absolutely terrified. I wonder
who she was and I've always wanted to thank her for
stepping forward and being there.

Stephen, Kent

It was Christmas Day 2012, and my husband Gary
and I were staying with our daughter. The two of us
went for a pre-lunch walk around a large cemetery and
I suddenly realised that Gary was having a stroke. We
had stupidly left our mobile phones behind, so I shouted
loudly for help, and the assistance we received was quite
overwhelming. I remember a tall man whose father had
died two weeks earlier and he stayed with my husband
and calmed him. There was also a young father who had
come with his wife to visit their eight-year-old daughter
who had died two years before; his wife called for the
ambulance, and they were all kindness itself. Gary made
a fairly good recovery and I just want to say thank you.

Sheila, Somerset

In 1945 I was four years old and lived at Strawberry Fields, a children's home in Liverpool. My parents had split up and my father had taken the two oldest children and my mother the two youngest. She couldn't cope very well so my sister and I found ourselves in this Salvation Army home. I was completely disorientated, feeling very alone, and in the playground I fell and I cut my knee quite badly. The people that came to my aid were two young builders who were working in the school playground. They had some putty and they devised a game for me and magically found these ball bearings in the putty. I remember my astonishment at seeing the ball bearings, and they kept hiding them to keep me amused and distract me from my troubles. I felt utterly lost and friendless and have never forgotten those two young men. Even now the smell of putty brings back that memory – and I still have the scar on my knee – thank you for your kindness.

Maureen, Suffolk

In September 2011 I suffered a major coronary while I was in hospital. At about two o'clock in the morning, I understand, the crash team came in and they pummelled my chest. I know how much they must have pummelled it because I had very bruised ribs when I came to. Later in the day, the doctor who had led the crash team came and stood against my bed, and she said that she was glad to see me still alive. I was furious with her, really angry, I said 'Why didn't you let me die? I was dying painlessly and look what you've done. I am a Christian, I'm not afraid to die.' It took me over a year to come to terms with the fact that I was still alive, and that I could be healthy and I could enjoy life. Now I have got to the point where I want to say sorry to that poor doctor, and thank you very much for giving me the opportunity to enjoy my wife, my home and my family and the things that I can do in retirement.

Ian, Devon

A few years ago I received a phone call at my desk to say that my husband had collapsed on the train. Fortunately I was only a few minutes away so I ran to the station. There were a number of people milling around, paramedics and station staff and so on, and out of the corner of my eye I noticed a lady sitting quietly on one of the seats on the train. When the paramedics eventually decided my husband could be moved to an ambulance, this lady got up and retrieved her coat. It turned out that when my husband had first collapsed she had taken off her coat and made a pillow for him to make him more comfortable. Amidst all the confusion I never really got the chance to thank this lady properly for her small act of kindness and consideration.

Sally, Essex

In 1963, at the age of 23, I was about to take up a job in Nigeria, but first I had to have various vaccinations. I reported to the Hospital for Tropical Diseases and was asked what I needed: I said, 'Yellow fever, cholera, smallpox and TB'. They promptly gave me all four, one after the other, but they didn't tell me that I might feel ill. I went back to work where my boss decided we were going to reorganise the bookshelves – not the easiest afternoon! I then walked to the Tube where as usual I had to stand. Not surprisingly I started to feel very ill, so I tapped the knee of a gentleman in a bowler hat and pinstripes and told him I was about to faint. I must have looked pretty awful as he leapt up and gave me his seat and all the passengers kept peering at me. The kind man asked where I was going and said he would get off the train at my station and take me home by taxi. This he did, leaving me at my door, and finished his journey in the taxi. I spent the evening huddled in front of the fire while my flatmates enjoyed the farewell party I had arranged. I would like to thank my rescuer and let him know that I spent four very happy years in Nigeria with no illness!

Gill, Wiltshire

One Sunday morning in August 1974, I was a week overdue with a baby, and I was admitted as an emergency to Stone Park Hospital in Beckenham, Kent. A West Indian ward sister met me and it transpired that in fact the baby had died. The nurse was supposed to be going off duty, but instead she stayed with me throughout the whole day, until the early evening. My husband was with me but we were both so shocked. I have always regretted that I never went back to the hospital, found out who she was and thanked her. I really want to thank her now.

Penny, West Sussex

I would like to thank the man who stood next to my 20-year-old son in a bank queue in Malawi and, noticing that he didn't look at all well, told him that he should go straight away to the hospital as he thought that he might have malaria. My son followed his advice and got speedy treatment for malaria and made a total recovery. Had this man not spoken up, my son would have been on the back of a truck going up country for hours on unmade roads, and the outcome could have been very different. Thank you that man!

Nan, Kent

In September 2013 my husband Seán, who had
been recovering from a stroke, went for a jog
along the narrow country road we live on and he
didn't come back. What had happened was that
he felt he was going to suffer an epileptic fit, and
the next thing he knew he had a woman literally
on top of him (as he puts it!), trying to turn him
into the recovery position. There was another
woman there, and they were obviously speaking
to him, asking who he was, but sadly he had lost
the power of speech. They very kindly called an
ambulance. We just really wanted to know who
these really kind people were. A few weeks later
we very happily discovered the kind Samaritans
were two neighbours who live half a mile up the
lane in the other direction and I'm so grateful to
them for stopping and looking after Seán.

Morag, Somerset

I was coming home from work on a Friday afternoon and I passed out at the wheel. I was coming out of a relatively minor road but onto a major junction. Apparently I bounced off all the cars on the way up and wrote off about eight of them! It was a type of epilepsy that I'd not had before. I was heading into a major intersection and somebody leapt through the window of the car and turned the engine off. I don't know who it was and ever since then I have really wished I could thank them. I woke up to find paramedics leaning over me. I am so grateful to the man concerned; it was incredibly brave and certainly saved my life.

Helen, Northamptonshire

I would like to thank Janet Bayford who assisted me in February 1988 following a scaffolding collapse in Camden Town, London. The top of my head was shattered by a pole and I stayed in hospital for 18 months before being discharged in a wheelchair. I'm still in the wheelchair, but I'm alive, well, and making something of my life again. Police reports say that Janet ran out of a nearby office into a very distressing scene. She climbed into the van and gave me comfort and assistance while I was unconscious. I did try and track her down but to no avail. I would still love to meet her and thank her personally.

Tony, London

In December 1994 I was at Lakeside Shopping Centre at Thurrock. It was pouring with rain and, as I entered a toy shop looking for a toilet, I slipped and turned my ankle. I sat on the toilet seat, with my knickers round my ankles, and the pain caused me to faint. Falling forwards, I snapped off my top four front teeth at the gums on the door lock and fell to the floor, suffocating myself with the crook of my arm. I could easily have died. Fortunately for me, there was a lady in the next cubicle who looked over the dividing partition and, having failed to force the door open because I was jamming it shut, climbed over the wall between the cubicles, and pulled my arm away from my nose and mouth, enabling me to breathe. She shouted for help, got me flat on the floor to recover from the faint and clean up my bloody mouth, and then asked for an ambulance to be called. Outside as she left, she told my husband what had happened, and then disappeared. After being cleaned up in hospital I tried unsuccessfully to find her. It took five years to get my teeth reconstructed and ever since then I have wanted to find the angel who saved my life to thank her.

Julie, Cambridgeshire

In October 2012 I was cycling home from work. I wasn't feeling very well, I was very tired, and so I thought I would bail out and take a taxi home. I put my bike in the back of the taxi, and the taxi driver looked at me and said 'Are you all right?' I said 'No, I'm not feeling well', and he said 'I think you're having a stroke, I think you should go to A&E.' After he said it the third time, I thought it must be serious, so I said I would. Two days later I was told I wasn't having a stroke, but that I really needed to see a heart specialist, and within six weeks I was having open-heart surgery with a new heart valve put in. It is hard to believe how my life changed at that point. People don't always say nice things about cab drivers, but this one saved my life. I'd also like to say that the medical profession in this country are incredible.

Tony, London

Just before Christmas in 2012, I woke up early in the morning with severe abdominal pain so my wife drove me down to A&E. They couldn't quite tell what the problem was but they just knew they needed to operate. The next thing I knew was someone was telling me that I'd had a cardiac arrest. I was lying in the surgical ward some days later and a doctor came in and he just looked at me and said, 'The last time I saw you, you were flat on the ground. You've been given a second life.' I never really got a chance to say thank you, and I'm trying to make the most of my second life, and God bless you.

James, London

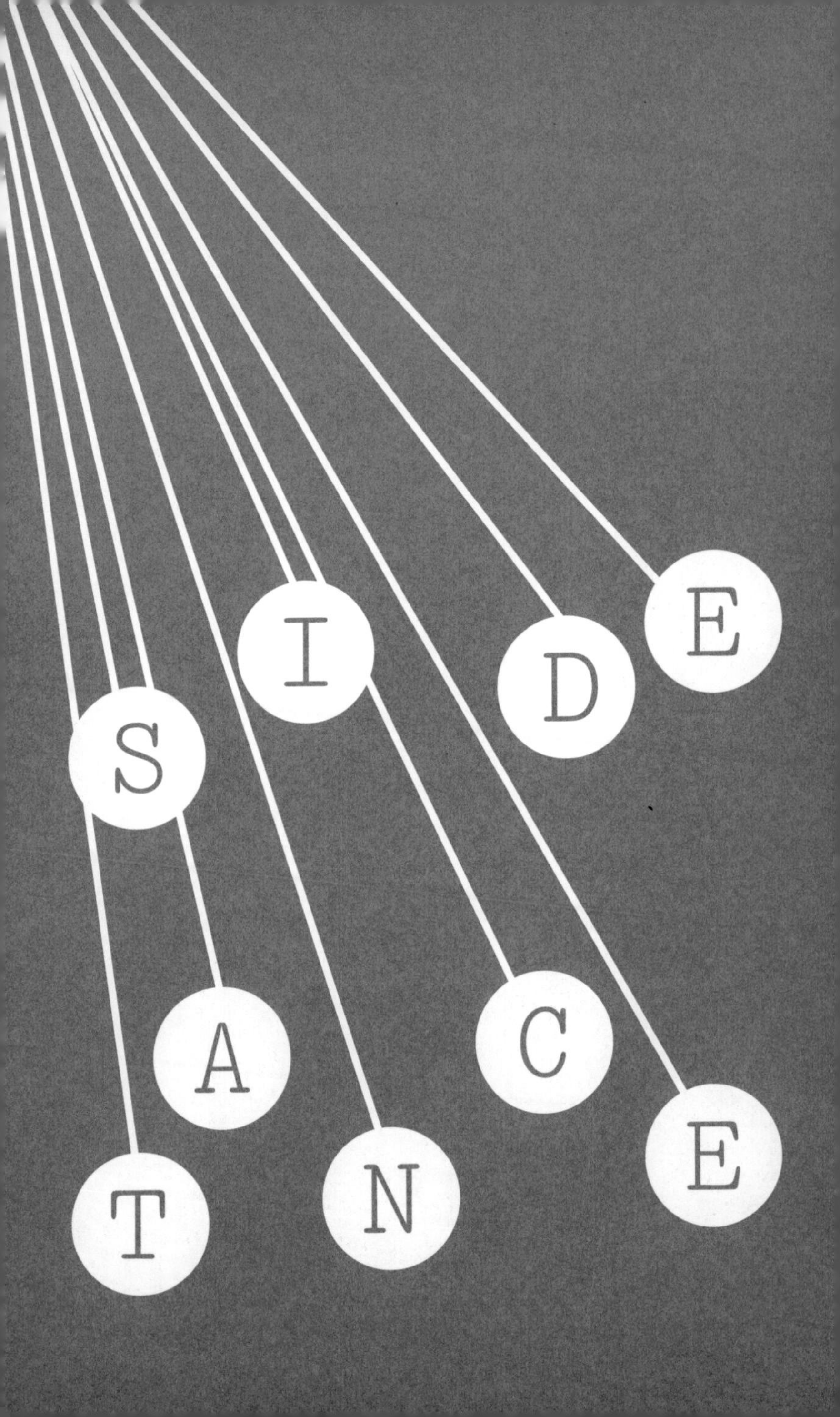
S I D E
T A N C E

'Gratitude is not only
the greatest of virtues,
but the parent of
all others.'

CICERO

Our roads are often dangerous,
unfriendly and often downright
scary places to be, so it is
heart-warming to know that
there are people out there who
really do want to help us when
we get into trouble, and we
don't need to have breakdown
cover to qualify. But as well
as the wonderful people who
helped these contributors pick
up their lost luggage, rescued
a child locked inside a car,
or fixed an accelerator arm
with a pair of tights, there
were others who were assisted
by kindly train and bus drivers
and passers-by.

I was walking my dog in a field that was quite overgrown with grass. When I returned to my car I discovered I had lost my car keys and I also had no mobile phone with me. This meant I had a 3-mile (5km) walk home and while I was resting outside a pub, which was closed because it was an Easter Monday, a young lady came round the corner and asked me if I knew directions to a shop that might have something she could buy for a picnic. I asked if she was in a hurry, which she was, and she went back to her car. Almost immediately she returned and asked me what my problem was. She then gave me a lift back to my home to collect my spare car keys and ran me back to the car park so I could continue to travel to watch my son play in a sports festival. I don't know her name but I thank her very much for being such a good Samaritan.

Karen, Surrey

* * * * * * * * * * * * * * * * * * *

Back in the early 1970s when I was 17 I went on a rather wild Greyhound Bus trip across the USA with a Swedish girl of the same age. We had everything carefully planned, and when we hit Albuquerque we had planned to get off the bus and stay overnight at the bus station, so that we could catch another bus early the next morning. The bus arrived at Albuquerque at 11 o'clock at night and we gathered our rucksacks and made our way to the door. But the bus driver stopped us and asked us what our plans were. When we told him that our intention was to sleep in the bus station he refused to let us get off: he clearly knew more than we did about overnight stays at Greyhound Bus stations and said that wasn't sure that we'd be safe and he just couldn't, with a clear conscience, let us get off the bus. We argued and argued with him, but he refused point blank to open the door so we had no choice – we had to stay on the bus until the next morning! Of course, I have no way of knowing what would have happened to us, but I've thought about that bus driver so many times over the years, and would love to be able to thank him for being so protective, and for saving us from whatever fate awaited two young, naïve European girls.

Annabel, Wiltshire

While getting out of my car outside The Cut, a small arts centre in Halesworth, Suffolk, to attend a drawing class, my wheelchair slipped and I ended up on the gravel with my legs in the car, unable to get in or out properly, or up off the ground. A gentleman called Ken spotted the problem and went inside to get help, returning with another man and his dog. They tried to lift me back into the chair without success, and a third man passing by, stepped up to help lift my legs and restore me to my chair. I did not catch the other two gentlemen's names and, although I did thank them at the time, would like to say thank you again. It was an awkward position to be in and I was extremely grateful for their help.

Simon, Norfolk

In 2003 my partner, who was pregnant, died in a car accident on the A5. We were ten weeks away from having a baby daughter. While she was trapped in the car, an upsetting scene, a Macmillan nurse who was just passing got in the car with my partner, sat beside her, held her hand and spoke to her just in case she could hear anything. I was told she stayed there for about an hour. I remember at the time my whole world had fallen apart and it really comforted me to think that human beings could be so wonderful. It was such a tremendous act of human kindness and I want to say thank you.

Jason, Essex

One dark, cold November morning in November 1990, I was mugged at Clapham High Street Station in South London. A young man walked up to me on the empty platform and sprayed mace in my eyes before making off with my bag. I screamed and then, terrified and in pain, I staggered out of the station onto the street. I approached a milkman who simply told me to call the police, but while I was wandering blindly around, a young woman suddenly appeared. She been in bed at the time, but had heard my scream, pulled on her dressing gown and come out to help. She put her arm around me and led me to an all-night cafe and got me a mug of tea before calling the police. Then she sat with me, not only until they arrived, but also until the ambulance came to take me to hospital. I expect I thanked her as I got into the ambulance but I don't remember.

I later asked the police for her phone number but it was never forthcoming. I've always wanted to thank her and tell her how very kind she was.

Charmian, London

It was 1978 and our daughter Mary was nine months old. I left work one day, picked Mary up and drove home. In those days it was possible to lock the car door manually: you didn't need a key to do it. I got out and I found that I was outside on the pavement, Mary was in the car with the key, and the door between us was locked. I think I'd started to panic at this stage – I found a brick in my front garden and tried to throw it at the window but it didn't work. A little crowd gathered on the pavement and I went into the house to try and get some help. Then, while I was in the house, a lorry driver was driving past, saw the commotion, managed to get into the car and got Mary out. By the time I came out he was gone. I have no idea who this man was after more than 30 years, but I'd like to say thank you for getting Mary out of the car that day.

Barbara, London

It was about 1970 and I was on a hitchhiking
holiday in Italy. At the time my brother and I ran an
import/export business between Rome and London.
I had to get back from Rome to London as soon as
possible, so I went to the slip road to the motorway,
and waited for about five or six hours to no avail.
Then, all of a sudden, a British car stopped. I asked
for London, the driver (who was Italian) agreed
without a second thought and he took me, not only
to London, but to the door of the house in Stepney
Green where I was living at the time. It was one
of the wonders of my life. I didn't thank that chap
enough, and I still can't thank him enough.

Robert, Wiltshire

In the 1960s my father, a disabled RAF ex-serviceman, and I had planned a journey from Salford to Sussex: me by pushbike and Dad in his motorised invalid trike. After a few miles Dad's clutch plate had disintegrated, dispersing bolts, springs and washers over the miles we had covered. I miraculously found the missing clutch plate springs, which I managed to refit, but had missed one necessary bolt. A passer-by told me about a garage; he thought it had been closed for some time, but I decided to give it a try. When I got there, a man in dirty overalls found me a bolt and kindly cut it to size, refusing all in return but my thanks. Once we were back home, I visited the garage again, but it was closed and had been for years! Whoever the mystery mechanic was, thank you.

Leslie, Merseyside

One bitterly cold day all the passengers on the bus on which I was travelling to my art class were asked to leave it before my destination. I saw a man getting into his car and I thought I would ask him for a lift, which I did. He agreed and I got in and off we went. When we reached my destination I got out and said 'That really was your good deed for the day.' And he said, 'Oh yes it was, because actually I was going the other way!' I was so surprised I wonder whether I actually thanked him or not.

Liz, Greater London

I would like to thank the kind couple that let me live on their drive for three months. I'd been accepted onto a PGCE course at Exeter University, but didn't have enough money to pay for accommodation, and had decided to try living in my van. The problem was going to be avoiding parking tickets so I knocked on a door at random and asked the lady who answered if she minded me parking outside her house. She went one step further and invited me to park on her drive and gave me a key to her garage so I'd have access to water. Thanks to this act of kindness I had a stable and secure place to call home and concentrate on my course. I met my wife during my studies and I've now been teaching for 13 years and feel lucky to be doing a job I love. I regret the fact that, after three months on that driveway, excited about the prospect of moving into a real house, I upped and left, without a word of thanks for the kind couple. Now is my chance: thank you.

Josh, Somerset

Two of us were walking home along the A23 in Surrey and we passed a broken-down car with a couple sitting in it; the weather was cold, wet and miserable, as were the couple. Their car had just died so they had no engine and no heating. We shared a house with several guys who had a lot of mechanical knowledge so we said that when we got home we would see if anyone could help. Two of our housemates said they would see what they could do, so we drove back to the broken-down car, armed with a Thermos of hot coffee and a packet of chocolate biscuits. We diagnosed that the problem was a faulty coil, and one of the guys had an old banger from which he could remove the coil and use it to replace the faulty one. So we drove the couple to our house where they were able to warm up, then the experts drove back to the broken-down car, fitted the replacement coil and drove the car back to our house, ready for the couple to continue their journey to London. All we asked was that they send us back our coil once they had had a new one fitted. So what happened then? Nothing. No coil was returned and that was the last we heard of it. Not every story ends as you would hope!

Bill, Kent

I was 12 years old in 1957 when we escaped from Hungary, which was going through a revolution. My parents got a job in central London and I came up to visit them. I spoke practically no English and had no idea where I was. I started to cry and spotted a couple of gentlemen: one of them had a top hat on, the other one had a cloak. I stopped them and said as much as I could say in English, which was where I wanted to go, but of course I didn't understand their explanation. They very kindly hailed a taxi and paid the fare, and off I went to where my parents were. It was such an early experience during our time in this country, and I want to say a really big thank you to them.

Kati, Hungary

Some years ago, while driving through Maidstone, I tried to park my car on the pavement and did not see the 46cm (18in) drop beyond. Needless to say the front of my car crashed down and I got well and truly stuck. A few minutes later, four young men that we would now describe as 'hoodies' came along and, without saying anything, they heaved and struggled until the car was back on firm ground, and then just went on their way. I truly cannot thank them enough and now see goodness in all our young people, whatever they're wearing.

Camelia, Kent

In 1986 I was staying in a grand old hotel in the centre of Moscow in what was then the Soviet Union. My mother had joined me for the weekend but was in a modern hotel on the outskirts of the city. I'd had a strange phone call in my hotel room the night before and I was told by some Swiss businessmen that the KGB checked, nightly, that you were where you should be. One evening, following a rowdy vodka session in the bar of my mother's hotel, I rushed off to get back to my own hotel to find the Metro shut and locked. I persuaded the armed guard to let me down the long static escalator onto the deserted platform, but there was no sign of any trains. After a couple of minutes, an empty train came through on its way home. I instinctively stuck out my hand and gradually the engine came to a halt at the end of the platform. Unbelievably, the guard stepped out and beckoned to me. We shared no common language but the train dropped me off at the square next to my hotel, to which I was escorted by another armed guard, at the train guard's request. I am so grateful to those men for getting me back to where, in the KGB's eyes, I was supposed to be.

Hannah, Bristol

In the late 1970s, I was an emergency-duty social worker. I was coming off duty at about 1am on New Year's Day. The weather was bad and the snow and ice caused me to skid off the motorway onto the verge. I ended up with two wheels on the ridge of the incline at the side of the motorway and two wheels in mid-air. I was terrified – there was no one around and I needed to get home to my husband and three young children. Mobile phones were a thing of the future so all I could do was pray! Then a man in white appeared, took over the controls of the car, and got me back on the road. To this day I cannot explain what happened. I got home to my sleeping husband and woke him with the words 'Tonight I have seen an angel'. He said, 'Did you dear?' and went back to sleep, but I made sure he heard the story a few times after that.

Pat, Norfolk

At the end of the 1970s I had just finished a PhD at the University of Essex in Colchester. I had got married three years earlier and my wife and I were heading back to Ireland. We drove up through England to catch the ferry at Holyhead and just outside Birmingham we had a puncture. We searched in our boot to discover that we had no tools and no jack, and the only thing I could think of was to take out my UK road map, and on the back it I wrote, in big black letters, 'Anyone please help, we need a jack!' A young chap, the same age as ourselves, stopped his car on the busy motorway (he was on his way to work), and not only offered us the use of the jack, but happily changed the tyre for us. We thanked him, caught our ferry, and arrived back in Ireland after one of the happiest periods of our young married life. But the thought still lingers – would that man from Birmingham, all those years ago, remember the good turn he did us on that cold and frosty morning?

Ciaran, Dublin

We were on our way to the theatre in London. I hadn't been up to the city for quite a while and, being a wheelchair user, I was quite terrified about the prospect. The only thing that really thwarted us were the kerbs – we just couldn't find a place to easily get up and down them. Suddenly out of nowhere, three chaps came and lifted me up in the air and got us over the hurdle. Being a rural dweller I'd always thought city people were a bit stand-offish but I was overwhelmed that weekend by everybody helping out. So I'd like to extend a really big thank you to those strangers for making the weekend such a success.

Caroline, Suffolk

In the early 1970s, after the death of my husband, I was driving north on the A1 with two small children and I had a puncture in my decrepit old Mini. I knew perfectly well how to change a wheel, having lived and worked in the African deserts for some years, but I was un-able to loosen the nuts. Out of the swirling lorries that passed me came a cheerful man who was a real boost to my spirits. He kindly changed the wheel, and when I tried to thank him he said, 'Oh, don't worry love, you do the same for me sometime.' You can imagine what an enormous help it was that this total stranger so kindly stopped at a time when I was at a very low ebb in life. I'd say keep doing it for other people because it made a huge difference to me. Thank you.

Jan, Hertfordshire

I was driving late at night sometime in November 1968. I was heading west on the A5 close to the junction with the A41, near Shifnal, Shropshire. I was in my black Morris 1000, and the road was very quiet, when I caught up with a heavily laden articulated goods lorry. I wanted to keep up my momentum and so rashly decided to overtake. I pulled out, and got as far as the rear wheels of the lorry's trailer, when the lorry started to move out into my lane and flash his indicators. The air in my car turned blue as I braked and moved back behind the lorry, just in time to see the flash of a car travelling at high speed in the opposite direction. The quick thinking of the lorry driver prevented a very nasty accident. I have been driving for 50 years now and – touch wood – I still have a blemish-free licence. My driving that night was out of character and I still reflect on what might have happened, so thank you Mr Lorry Driver.

Martin, Devon

I like to say thank you to a Kikuyu family in Kenya who rescued me one evening, over 30 years ago, when I was about 20. I was on my own, driving from the Mount Kenya area to Nairobi in my little white Mini, when I got a puncture. It was on a Sunday evening, it was already dark and the road was quite deserted. I couldn't believe it and continued to drive as best I could until I had to stop. I knew I was in a dangerous situation but I had no alternative but to flag down the first car that came by. It was driven by a man with several people in the car and he was nothing but kindness. He changed the wheel and drove behind me to the nearest petrol station, which was quite a distance away, to see if they could fix my tyre. In the event I had destroyed the punctured tyre by driving on it for too long, but I will never forget the kindness of that family.

Robin, Surrey

Many years ago, I was in Waltham Cross, Hertfordshire, driving home from my parents' home, with three small children, a dog and, of course, no mobile phone. It was a cold, wet night and I had had to drive through a deep puddle. The next time I stopped the car, at a roundabout, the car died. I coasted around the corner, still on the roundabout but out of harm's way, and wondered what to do. A car pulled up behind me and two youths got out. 'Oh no', I thought, 'This is all I need.' As it turned out they were knights in shining armour! While we waited in the car they got under the bonnet (to dry out the spark plugs, I suppose), called up their friends on their CB radio to bring the right tools, and set about sorting it out. They clearly had a ball, although I don't think their girlfriends in the back of their car were very pleased. I was so unbelievably grateful but I never thanked them enough and never knew who they were. I will always think of them as heroes.

Clare, Oxfordshire

ACKNOWLEDGEMENTS

Thanking those involved in compiling a book already filled with heart-warming Thank Yous might seem like an overdone Oscar acceptance so I will be brief. While the redoubtable J.P. Devlin had the idea of introducing the concept of non-requited gratitude to the programme, Dixi Stewart ensured it became a regular feature and Maggie Olgiati routinely scoured the *Saturday Live* inbox for the best examples. Nicola Newman of Pavilion Books suggested the idea of compiling them into one uplifting and warm-hearted volume. Katie Hewett did a wonderful job in choosing from the many Thank You stories the programme broadcast. For the BBC, Danielle Hammond offered contractual advice while *Saturday Live*'s newest recruit Olivia Cope made contact with nigh-on 150 listeners, requesting permission to include their stories. And on behalf of all of us at *Saturday Live*, a loud thank you, to the people who said 'thank you'.

Andrew Smith
Editor, *Saturday Live*
BBC Radio 4

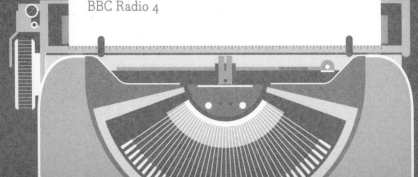

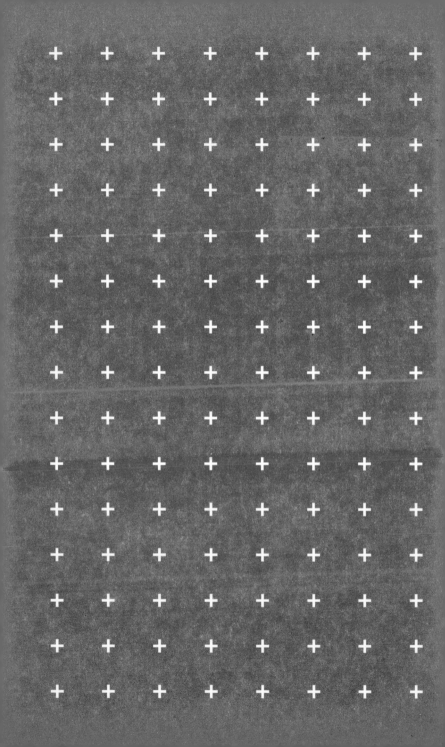